THE SN

Adam Lively was born in Swansea in 1961 and studied history and philosophy in England and America. He has published two novels, *Blue Fruit* (1988) and *The Burnt House* (1989), and a pamphlet in Chatto Counterblasts series, *Parliament: The Great British Democracy Swindle* (1990). His work has also appeared in the anthologies *20 Under 35*, *P.E.N New Poetry II* and *The Dylan Companion*.

His new novel, *Sing the Body Electric*, will be published in June 1993 the year in which he was selected as one of The Best of Young British Novelists.

He lives in London with his wife Diana, and their son Jacob.

Adam Lively

THE SNAIL

VINTAGE

VINTAGE
20 Vauxhall Bridge Road, London SW1V 2SA

London Melbourne Sydney Auckland Johannesburg
and agencies throughout the world

First published by Hutchinson, 1991

Vintage edition 1993

2 4 6 8 10 9 7 5 3 1

Printed and bound in Great Britain by
Cox & Wyman, Reading, Berkshire

ISBN 0 09 930358 2

To Vera and Rachel

Contents

Acknowledgements

The following books provided valuable information on the sinking of the *Arandora Star* and the treatment of refugees during the Second World War: Bernard Wasserstein, *Britain and the Jews of Europe 1939–1945* (Clarendon Press, 1979), and Peter and Leni Gillman, *'Collar the Lot!' How Britain interned and expelled its wartime refugees* (Quartet, 1980).

I

The Show Begins

THE LIGHTS DIM. The curtains, a river of blood from ceiling to floor, slide slowly apart. A fanfare bursts into the darkness, and suddenly the screen is illuminated. Antonín's eyes are wide open, buckets into which the light is being poured. He looks down the row at the other upturned faces bathing in the flickering glow and, for the first time since coming to England, he feels safe. There is a warm fug of damp clothing and musty upholstery. He sinks down into his seat, losing himself in the smothering, people-filled darkness.

Beside him, his Uncle Stefan gazes impassively at the newsreel. His watery blue eyes reflect the quickly cutting scenes of tanks and columns. A muttering starts up around them. Those of their party who understand English are whispering translations impatiently to their neighbours. It is March 1939. The news they are watching is of the invasion of their homeland.

After the newsreel comes the main feature. The muttered, excited conversations around them continue to spread. Even when they have run out of words — sat back to allow the flickering light and shadows to dance across their faces – they continue to gesticulate, their hands jerking up and turning in gestures of helpless disbelief.

No one gives Antonin a translation – not even his uncle, who understands English perfectly. In the feature film, Englishmen walk in and out of rooms, addressing each other in their strange language, with its ugly, twisted vowels. Towards the end, two men chase each other at night through the streets of a city. For a moment the faces of the audience are shrouded in shadow. The two men fall, there is a struggle on the shiny wet tarmac, then one of them pulls himself up and runs. With his coat flapping like broken wings, he disappears into the darkness.

When the film is finished, the audience stand for the British national anthem. The tune makes Antonin think of a funereal waltz danced by some large, ponderous animal. He whispers this to his uncle, and his uncle gives a wistful smile. This is the closest his uncle ever gets to laughing.

The Czechs shuffle out on to the street, where the headlights of the taxis and buses sweep across the crowds on the pavement like the ever-shifting light of the projector in the cinema. Still discussing the newsreel, they are piled into cars and driven across London. In the lofty reception room of a Georgian terrace house they are given a cold buffet by a disapproving butler and two maids. Despite the newsreel, perhaps because of it, their mood is almost festive. They talk about the coming war, the parts that they hope to play in it. For once, there is a feeling of solidarity.

Antonin, not yet sixteen years old, is sensitive to this mood. For the first time, he feels accepted by them. For the first time he moves through them easily. None of them are practising their halting English now. He feels cocooned by the familiar, loved language that surrounds him. Some of them even bother to stop and talk to him, to ask him about his family and the home he has left behind. This they have never done before.

When it is time to leave, and the cars that will take them back out of London are drawn up in the road outside, Antonin lingers on the steps of the house. He is clinging to the last scraps of the evening. From the top of the steps he can see down the street opposite to a row of wide-windowed shops, before which a crowd throngs back and forth, the headlights flashing across them. The night is filled with voices, horns, engines. He stares desperately around, pressing these last images to his mind. In his hand Antonin clutches the piece of paper he was given in case he got separated from the group. It bears the address of this house.

He will jealously guard that piece of paper and the memory of that magical evening through the long, empty months in the country house with the other Czechs, through the wet weeks in the lodging-house in the Midlands where he and his uncle are sent after the war breaks out, and through the sleepless days and nights with the English family to whom he is taken when his uncle is sent to prison. When he finally runs away from the English family (bullying father, cold mother, smirking children) it is for London that he makes. Slowly, with money he has stolen from the English family, he makes his way up through the southern suburbs, showing the address to strangers and gathering what he can from their meaningless gabble and impatient gestures. Fortunately it is warm and at night he can sleep in the air-raid shelters. For by now the Blitz has begun.

Until, one September afternoon, he is standing on those steps again. He squints into the sunlight, down the street opposite, to the row of wide-windowed shops. A man in shirtsleeves has been standing there, watching him, ever since he arrived an hour before. The man has been pretending to do other things – wait for a bus, look at the displays in the windows – but Antonin knows that really he has been watching him. He is scared of being caught and taken back to the bullying father, cold mother and smirking children. He goes back up the steps and knocks on the door again. Crouching at the letter box, he shouts through it 'Hey, hello!' He can see a table in the hall with a sheet over it. The place is still and empty. He looks up at the boarded windows, knocks again. He stands at the door for nearly half an hour, banging on it every couple of minutes, then sits down on the steps. Shirtsleeves is still waiting over by the shops. Antonin moves to the steps of the house next door, which is hidden from the shops by a corner.

The warm afternoon draws on. Some people hurry down the street in ones and twos. He watches shirtsleeves walk past once, pretending not to look at him. Then the sirens start riding their roller-coaster up and down the street. The people disappear. The sirens stop. Nothing happens for a long time. Then, out of the eerie silence, comes a burst of muffled thuds as the guns open up somewhere on the other side of the river. Antonin immediately stands and looks out across the roofs towards the pale orange flicker of evening sunlight on one of the grey barrage balloons. He is scared. Even shirtsleeves has left his post on the corner of the street, where he has been pretending to wait for a bus, glancing up at the sky every now and then as though expecting rain. Now the streets are like an empty stage set waiting for something to happen. Down below him, Antonin notices a basement door. He clanks down the iron steps into the area and pushes it open. Inside, dimly, he sees some mattresses, and a table and chairs beside one of the iron pillars that prop up the low ceiling. He calls out 'Hey, hello!' No reply. The darkness envelopes him as he shuts the door. In the distance the anti-aircraft guns thump randomly.

Hours later, curled up on one of the mattresses, the boy is woken by boots clanking down the iron steps. Three people burst through the door into the pitch-black basement.

The Snail

He can tell there are three of them – two men and a woman – by their voices. They laugh and joke in the darkness, stumbling across the room. They sound drunk. Outside it is quiet, until suddenly there is a burst of anti-aircraft bangs nearby and then the shuddering crump of a bomb. It must have fallen only a couple of streets away because Antonin can hear it dent the ground. One of the people swears and then they are quiet for a while.

Antonin crouches, listening carefully for any movement they might make towards him. After a while they start talking together quietly. The things they say get shorter, and the spaces between them longer and longer. The darkness fills the spaces, pressing up against the boy's eyeballs as he strains for any glimmer of light. The mattress beneath him smells and is lumpy with broken springs. It is hard to keep his balance on it. His eyes continue to search, but the muscles in his limbs have begun to relax. Suddenly, his arm is grabbed, and before a scream can escape his mouth, a large fleshy hand, smelling of tobacco and drink, is pressed into his face.

II

One By One

ON THAT PARTICULAR day, I left work at about six and beat my usual path from the Ministry of Information, across Tottenham Court Road to the Belgravia Tavern in Fitzroy Street. My job consisted of writing exhortations to the nation to be cautious, to stay at home, not to move from place to place during raids. Every night, when work was over, I ignored all my own instructions. The reason I liked the Belgravia was that it was frequented by the type of people who laughed at all that fussy, old-womanish propaganda. They were the type who wouldn't take the war seriously, the 'Soho non-blitzers'. The more threatening and serious things got, the greater for them became the laughable absurdity of the whole business. Many of them, like myself, had jobs that involved taking the war seriously. But as soon as we stepped through the doors of the Belgravia, we left all that behind.

The Belgravia was a small, enclosed world of its own, like an ocean-going liner sealed off from the storms outside by its blackout of plywood and black sateen. It sailed through the war on a sea of beer and ruthless frivolity, crammed

6

every night with back-scratching, back-stabbing revellers. Anybody who betrayed weakness by talking about the bombing – or perhaps just by appearing pensive for a moment – was ruthlessly cut down. It was a world of banter and gossip, with its own pecking order. At the centre of attention – and occupying the prime positions at the bar – were the full-time 'non-blitzers', a motley collection of aesthetes, shirkers and fly-by-nights who in one way or another had sidestepped total war. Only they could boast – eyeing their audience all the time for telltale signs of disapproval – that they were a positive drain on the war effort. Around this central core there were concentric rings of part-time 'non-blitzers' – some members of the outer rings in uniform – who admired and emulated the central core to varying degrees. I was somewhere on one of the outer rings of this strange galaxy, a tourist who visited because it provided an antidote to work and a way of filling up a rather empty life.

On this particular evening I was met at the bar by a cadaverous BBC man called Aubrey Taylor. If I was a minor planet on the outer edges of the Belgravian galaxy, Aubrey Taylor was like some small meteorite floating aimlessly through an inter-stellar vastness. He was visible only when illuminated by contact with one of the bigger stars. Not that he wasn't a strange-looking chap, if you did happen to notice him. His face looked as though it had been dragged downwards, with a nose that started delicately at the top and ended up hanging bulbously over a thin-lipped mouth. The mouth was set low down in his jaw, so that there was desperately little room between the bottom lip and the end of his chin. Only his darkly watchful eyes saved him from looking lugubrious.

'MacCready was looking for you earlier, Morgan,' was the first thing he said to me that evening.

Now MacCready was definitely one of the bigger stars, a

burly red-headed artist who people said was going to be a great sculptor one day.

'What did he want?' I asked, into my beer.

'I don't know. Perhaps he wants to do you in pipe-cleaners.'

There were a lot of jokes doing the rounds at that time about MacCready's pipe-cleaners. He made animals and birds out of them which he tried to flog at exorbitant prices. Some of them were rather beautiful.

'Terrible racket last night, wasn't it?' said Taylor.

I shrugged. 'Didn't notice. In nirvana.' I raised my beer glass and nodded at it.

'Bloody dreadful. I went for a walk, God knows why. I wrote a poem about it. Here, have a look. I thought I might send it off to Penguin New Writing.'

Conversations with Taylor always seemed to proceed in this stilted, awkward manner, a stuttering sequence of petty misunderstandings, half-hearted stabs at humour and conversational gambits that even the speaker could scarcely be bothered to pursue. He laid his poem out on the counter beside us.

At this point I should say something about myself. I'm the type who can't bear to see people upset or unhappy. I hate offending anyone, because the consequences embarrass me and make me feel uncomfortable. I'm accommodating, but out of squeamishness rather than generosity. I'm what people call a 'soft touch'. Taylor had got it into his head a few months before that being a journalist, or at least a former journalist, I could advise him on his literary efforts, and even help to get them published. He seemed a rather sad character, so I went along with this, and ever since then had suffered a deluge of prose and poetry. His style was inflatedly romantic – doom-laden, weighed down with lurid imagery, and stuffed with philosophical and quasi-mystical intimations. All this – he liked explaining to me at inordinate length –

was 'a reflection of the times we live in'. In his longer pieces, Taylor went in for a particularly irksome brand of fantasy. He once presented me with a sixty-page verse epic that was like *The Ring of the Nibelung* rewritten by Edward Lear. His demands were becoming ever greater, so it was with misgivings that I picked up and read this latest offering.

AIR RAID

The snapped strings of sleep
Whiplash across the bleeding sky,
Bombs nail the city
To sods of broken earth;
The eye is nailed to the bone.
The ground pulls down the blue-black hood
That keeps us nailed
To this waning world.
The whining wind whips up a foam of fear,
While deep below flash by
The nun; the bright red worm;
The twitching haunch of beast.
Dreamlights pick out
The scuttles on the ocean floor.
It goes on:
Catastrophe
Disintegrates
To nothing again.
And now we will wait
For other deaths.
We will be visited,
Borne like this
On wings of fire
To gasping machines.

'Bit bloody gloomy, isn't it?' I handed it back.

Aubrey Taylor gave a lop-sided grin and said, 'I suppose it is.'

'Try John Lehmann if you like. I don't suppose the government will stick it on a poster as a morale booster.'

Taylor flushed with pride. Actually I thought it was a pretty rotten poem – portentous, disjointed and alliterative. I was about to tell him as much when he glanced over my shoulder and said, 'There's MacCready now.'

I looked round. MacCready, pushing his way through the pub, had the physical presence of an actor playing a medieval baron. The crowd parted for him.

'Where have you been, Morgan? This Anglo-Saxon been boring you, again?' His freckled, boyish face beamed at me as he pulled up a stool and undid his heavy, stained raincoat. From the pockets he took out some of his pipe-cleaner animals, put them on the bar and said 'So who's going to give me some money? A shilling each.'

The animals had got squashed in his pocket. Delicately he pulled them back into shape with his fleshy fingers.

'A shilling?' I said. 'That's bloody outrageous.'

'But the beauty of these is that you can change them later if you get bored of them. It's a new concept in sculpture. There.'

He leaned back to look at them. The five animals stood in a row, as though about to enter a pipe-cleaner ark. At the back was the biggest and most elaborate: a giraffe made from perhaps twenty pipe-cleaners, with an elaborately plaited neck and one of its back legs wittily cocked like a dog. In front of that came an elephant with a long, baroque trunk, and a snake that MacCready had arranged so that it was slithering over the rim of an ashtray. Then there was a monkey swinging from a branch, and at the front something that I couldn't at first identify consisting of elegant swirls topped by a strange horned head.

'What's that one supposed to be?' I asked.

'A snail.'

'I'll give you ninepence for it,' I said, and counted out the coppers.

'I always thought you were a man of taste and refinement,' said MacCready when he'd bought himself a beer. 'Perhaps you'd like to start a collection. I do commissions.'

'I thought you were going to do Morgan,' put in Aubrey Taylor, 'when you said you were looking for him.' MacCready smiled condescendingly at him between gulps of his beer, and encouraged by this Taylor ploughed on. 'I've been meaning to ask you: where on earth do you get all those pipe-cleaners from? Fell off the back of a lorry, I suppose? I'm surprised the government still allows their manufacture, with all that wire inside. They're taking away all the park railings, you'd think they'd do something about pipe-cleaners, wouldn't you?'

MacCready suddenly slammed his glass down on the counter, stood up and kicked his stool away. He was famous for his tantrums. The drinkers along the bar stopped talking and turned to watch. For a few moments he just stood there, red-faced and glaring at poor Aubrey Taylor. Then he grabbed the giraffe off the counter and, holding it up in front of Taylor's face, started pulling it apart and refashioning it. The legs and body were yanked up over the neck, so that the whole thing formed a kind of obscene tower. Then the head was pulled apart into a bulbous knob, and two more protuberances formed to hang where the haunches had been. The pub looked on, fascinated.

'What's that, MacCready?' asked Taylor, watching him nervously. 'What are you making?'

MacCready furiously put the finishing touches, then shoved it into Aubrey Taylor's hands. 'Winston's cock,' he yelled and stormed across the pub, stopped, came back, grabbed my arm, and frogmarched me to the door.

'Sorry about that,' said MacCready cheerfully when we

were outside. 'Some of these Englishmen have no manners.' He leant over me, breathing beery breath.

'That's all right,' I said, irritated with all this Celtic camaraderie. I moved back towards the door of the pub.

'Wait.' MacCready held my arm. 'I wanted to talk to you about something. You speak languages, don't you? Weren't you a foreign correspondent?' I nodded. 'Well, you might be able to help us then. We had an intruder at our place a couple of nights ago. We think he might be foreign. I thought you could talk to him, find out who he is.'

'What kind of intruder?'

'A boy, about sixteen or seventeen. Quite a pretty one, a Jew.' He smiled lasciviously. MacCready liked trying to shock people by pretending to be homosexual.

'I suggest you take him along to the police. They'll find out who he is.' I didn't want to get mixed up in MacCready's capers.

'For Christ's sake, Morgan, you're sounding like that stupid Englishman. Why don't you come and have a look at him. He's a mystery. He might be a parachutist, or a Russian aristocrat on the run from Stalin.' He was still gripping my arm.

'Where is he now, this boy?'

'At the place where we're living, five minutes from here. He doesn't seem to have anywhere else to go. In fact he seems a bit confused.'

'All right then, but this had better not be some stupid joke.'

We started walking up the street, MacCready still holding my arm. By now I was quite curious to know what it was all about. I was also interested to see what kind of a place MacCready lived in. He had referred to 'we'.

As he had said, it was only a few streets away, just north of Oxford Street. A terrace of Georgian houses glowed in the evening sun. The air raid was late tonight. In front of the houses stood a row of To Let signs. Most of the windows were boarded up, the rich owners having left for overseas or the country. I stopped for a moment and looked at the terrace. There was something familiar about it.

MacCready and his friends, it turned out, were living in the basement of one of the more dilapidated buildings. I was led down some iron steps and into a low, dark basement with stone paving on the floor. It extended quite far back and I could just make out at the far end piles of old junk: wood, metal, some bits of plastic. Perhaps these were the materials for MacCready's sculptures. Around the walls were four or five mattresses, heaps of bedding, and an old sofa with the stuffing coming out. In the middle of the room was a table, at which sat a long-haired man, a woman who had once been pointed out to me in the Belgravia as MacCready's 'model', and the mysterious visitor.

'This is Morgan,' said MacCready. 'He's going to talk to the boy. Go on then, Morgan: ask him something in German.'

I had stopped dead still in the doorway, staring at the boy. 'He's not German,' I said. 'He's Czech.'

'How can you . . . ?' began the woman.

'So you do know him?' said MacCready.

Through my amazement at seeing Antonin Treiber sitting in this London basement, I registered MacCready's comment. It was a strange thing to say.

At that moment, the sirens started up.

III

Stories Are There To Be Told

BEFORE THE WAR, I had been the *News Chronicle*'s correspondent in Vienna. The paper had sent me there in February 1934, when Chancellor Dollfuss, under the guidance of Mussolini, had turned on the Austrian socialists. I was there in July when a group of Austrian Nazis occupied the Chancellory and murdered Dollfuss. And over the next four years I watched as the conservative and authoritarian Austrian leadership – with the acquiescence of Italy, France and Britain – gradually surrendered Austrian independence. I grew to hate the hypocrisy of those smooth, aristocratic Austrian politicians for whom anything could be glossed over by a 'gentlemen's agreement' couched in suitably elevated, diplomatic language. Then in March 1938, when Schuschnigg made a last, small gesture towards Austrian autonomy, Hitler's troops marched in and took over. A few weeks later, along with a number of other British and French journalists, I was ordered out.

Back in London, during the nervous celebrations surrounding Munich, I conceived a hatred for the British leadership as bitter as that I had had for the Austrian, and for similar reasons. When the war came, I presented myself for service – but aged forty, overweight and with bad eyes, I was turned down. With my fluency in German and knowledge of Austria, I had hoped and expected to be approached for Intelligence work. But the call never came. With hindsight it was easy to find reasons for this – my lower middle-class origins, for example, or my membership in the late twenties of the Independent Labour Party. I applied to the Ministry of Information and was given a job, though not an important or interesting one. I resented the fact that my considerable skills and experience were being under-used in the war effort.

One of my last acts before leaving Vienna was to help a Czech journalist acquaintance, a Jew, obtain British visas for his son and brother. Another instance of my squeamishness. Josef Treiber, an aloof man who found it distasteful to ask me for help, was convinced that Hitler was encouraging agitation by the Sudeten Germans in order to establish a pretext for the invasion of the whole of Czechoslovakia. He was also convinced that Jews in a German-controlled Czechoslovakia would be no safer than they were in Germany itself. His wife insisted on staying with him throughout, but Treiber was determined to get his only son and his elder brother away to safety. I arranged meetings with an official I knew at the British Embassy in Vienna and wrote to Peter Musgrave, a pro-Zionist Conservative MP who had interceded in similar cases in the past. I didn't hold out much hope for Treiber, because the embassy official had told me privately that the government feared an anti-Semitic backlash in Britain and was ordering its embassies to reduce the number of visas they granted. In addition, the security services had warned that the Germans could use Jewish emigration as a means of smuggling spies into the country. But Musgrave's influence must have helped, because the next thing I heard, once I was back in England, was that the uncle and nephew had got their visas and were being housed, along with a number of other Czech refugees, in Musgrave's mansion in Sussex.

I visited them there in the spring of 1939. The boy, Antonin, I had never seen before, and the uncle I had met just once, in a café in Vienna. Stefan Treiber was even more distant and difficult to fathom than his brother. He was fifty-five, but looked and moved more like a man ten years older. According to Josef, he had been a successful businessman in Germany, but in 1933 had been in a train accident in which he himself had been injured and a number of those around him killed. He had never recovered from this experience, and Josef had had to take over his affairs and sell his business. Stefan had never married. He was tall, with a stooped back and thinning grey hair. He didn't look in the least Jewish. He spoke excellent German and English, and told me at length, as we sat together in the chilly gloom of a servants' pantry, of the kindness he and his nephew had received since arriving in England, and of the beauty of the English countryside. But his flat voice told me that he was uninterested in what he was saying, that he was performing a duty and couldn't be bothered to disguise the fact. All the time, the boy gazed solemnly at us. He seemed to be hanging on our every word, though when I asked him questions in English and German, he didn't appear to understand either.

That was the last I saw of the Treiber uncle and nephew. On the outbreak of war, when enemy aliens were being interned, I made inquiries and discovered, to my surprise, that Stefan Treiber had been given Category A status, comprising those who were an actual or possible threat to the nation's security. The boy was in Category B, which meant that his movements were to be restricted. I had intended to lodge some kind of complaint about this, not least because despite Stefan Treiber's German connections, they were both Czech nationals. But the beginning of the war was a busy and chaotic time. I never got round to it.

Strange as this may sound, I wasn't surprised to find Antonin Treiber sitting in the fading light of MacCready's basement. To understand that, you have to imagine the times we were living through. It was a world where houses were turned inside out like discarded gloves, flinging lavatories, dressing tables and occupants into the street. The disturbed, chaotic motion of the human particles within the city was such that there could be no coincidence, because there was no normality. When beautiful September mornings were suffused with the sordid smell of leaking coal gas, it could seem quite natural that something you had been pushing comfortably to the back of your mind should suddenly spring forward and confront you. And that was the strangest part of the whole business: my overwhelming feeling on seeing Antonin Treiber was one of guilt.

'Well then,' said MacCready, 'say something to him in Czech.'

Ignoring him, I went up to the table and said in English, 'Do you remember me?' I put a finger to my chest and added, 'Henry Morgan.' The boy nodded.

'Little bastard,' said the long-haired man. 'He made out to us he didn't speak English.'

'Can you speak English?' I said.

The boy stared at me. He shrugged his shoulders and shook his head at the same time.

It was almost dark in the basement. The jolting thumps of the anti-aircraft guns had started. MacCready and the woman put boards in the small windows, wedging them in with old curtains. Then they lit candles. To distract us from the bombs, I told them the story of how I knew the boy.

'What happened to his parents?' asked the woman when I had finished.

I noticed for the first time how handsome she was, with her ruddy brown hair, strong jaw and clear blue eyes. I spent the rest of the night trying not to look at her too much.

'I don't know about the parents,' I said.

At six o'clock the next morning, when the all clear sounded, I walked the boy back to my flat near Kings Cross. I had no idea what to do with him, but he had clearly become my responsibility. Oxford Street had been blocked off and there were no buses running along Tottenham Court Road. We walked past streets crisscrossed with white tape. Groups of people stood behind the tape, looking at the bomb damage with excitement and interest. A stream of commuters passed them, coming from the mainline stations. I learnt, in scraps of half-remembered Czech, that Antonin had been staying with a family outside London. I could learn nothing as to what had brought him to MacCready's basement.

I bought him some food, left him at the flat and dragged myself to work. I was desperately tired. At my desk, the leaflets I had been working on floated up to me as though through deep water.

Make your family gargle before they make for the shelter: Make them gargle again when they return. *Don't spit: it is a dirty habit.* If you see anyone spitting, it is your duty to tell the warden at once.

I laid my head down and dozed, dreaming about MacCready's pipe-cleaner monkey swimming in a green sea. I jerked awake, and the papers on my desk floated up to me again. People brushed past my desk slowly like enormous fish drifting through tendrils of weed. I nodded back to sleep and saw a mass of stampeding animals lit in red. My eye was caught by hooves stamping in the dust, a tough-hided flank brushing close by.

I had intended to return straight to the flat after work, to check that the boy was all right. But there was always time for a quick beer at the Belgravia. My desk-top dreams had reminded me that I had left behind the pipe-cleaner snail I had bought from MacCready. I was damned if I was going to give MacCready ninepence for nothing. So at the end of another beautiful September day, as the shadows lengthened until they were creeping up the buildings on the other side of the street, I found myself crossing Tottenham Court Road again. And again Aubrey Taylor was waiting for me at the bar of the Belgravia.

'Hello, Morgan. MacCready was looking for you earlier.'

I looked into Taylor's expressionless face. It was a yellowish grey colour, patches of stubble sprouting through a sheen of grease and sweat.

'What did he want?'

'Something to do with that thing he sold you last night. I think the fellow's got a screw loose somewhere. You know what someone was telling me about him the other day . . .'

He talked on. There was an oppressive, monotonal droning in Taylor's voice when he got on to the subject of MacCready – like the ramblings of a religious fanatic or mass murderer. Recently I had noticed it more and more, and hoped that it might signal a switch in Taylor's obsessive attentions away from me. There was something claustrophobic about Taylor. I glanced at him again with distaste, remembering vaguely how a phrase of his poetry – 'the twitching haunch of beast' – had taken on a life of its own in my dream at the office.

'Sorry?' Taylor had asked me a question.

'I said, did you go round to MacCready's place last night? What's it like?'

'I don't know. We were going to go to another pub, but then the raid started so we went into a public shelter.'

Taylor suddenly changed tack, like a radio switching between stations. 'I did another poem today.'

'Not tonight, for goodness' sake, Taylor. All I want to do is have a quick drink and go home.'

'And find MacCready.'

'Who said I was looking for him?'

'He should be in later. He usually is. He likes my poems, you know. He told me.'

'I find that hard to believe.'

'He did. You and MacCready are the only ones who can stomach them. You see, I know that they're unpalatable. Who needs pretty elegies now? Do you think things are going to be better, even if we win?'

'I shouldn't start talking like that, Taylor. You'll get yourself into trouble.'

'We've reached a point of no return, the Apocalypse. The slope's getting steeper and steeper. Time's gathering itself up to hurl itself into the abyss.'

'For Christ's sake!' I swigged my beer. 'Can't you save that stuff for your blasted poems?'

Taylor smiled his usual sheepish smile. 'Sorry, Morgan. I've had a lot on my mind recently. The BBC have given me sick leave. None of all this really matters to me any more.' He flapped a hand in the direction of the door of the pub.

Somehow I didn't care to follow up this cryptic remark. I bought him another beer instead. An hour later we were both drunk. MacCready had still not turned up. 'Bugger it,' I said. 'I'm going to look for him.' The boy could wait a bit longer.

'I'll come with you.'

'Piss off, Taylor. Why don't you stay here and write some more of your bloody poems?'

'You won't be safe out there on your own.'

'It's none of your bloody business.'

'You don't realise. You need me.'

I pushed Taylor away and struggled through the crush of drinkers towards the door. I looked back once and saw Taylor starting after me. 'Bugger it,' I muttered and slammed the door behind me.

'Bugger it, bugger it,' I kept muttering as I tottered along the street. The darkness had enveloped me. Behind me the pub door opened and closed again. I started running, tripped after a few steps, and landed heavily on my side. I lay there panting, the world reeling around me. The beams of searchlights were fanning out across the sky. 'Thud-thud' went the barrage in the distance. 'Thud-thud' went my heart against my flabby chest. I sat up and listened. There were no footsteps following.

I walked on cautiously, trying to remember the way I had come with MacCready. The moon came out from behind clouds and for a moment I could make out the white lines marking the edge of the road. I was beating a diagonal path between them. When the moon disappeared again, I waved my arms stiffly in front of me as I walked.

I saw a glimmer of flames licking the darkness where incendiaries had fallen. Some had fallen harmlessly in the road, some on the roof of a terrace of shops. There were already a couple of wardens on the scene, the white 'W' on their helmets glowing weirdly in the green flames of the incendiaries as they stopped to smother them with sandbags. Above me I could still hear the drone of the bombers, like lorry engines perpetually straining up a hill. By the light of the burning roofs, I looked back and saw a man walking down the street towards me. He stopped and took shelter in a doorway when I turned round. I was standing by the terrace of Georgian houses to which MacCready had brought me the previous night. Above me was the street sign: Widlake Street W1.

It was only then, seeing the name, that I remembered when I had been here before. Peter Musgrave lived here. I had been here two years before, to thank him for interceding in the Treiber case. I had walked up this street from the bus stop beside the shops that were now burning behind me.

Twenty minutes later, after a very English interview, I had walked back again.

Now, by the light of the flames behind me and of the bombers' moon above, I walked up to Musgrave's house again. The windows were boarded. I went down to MacCready's basement, which was in the house next door, and found it empty and padlocked. An uncanny thought, barely more than a sequence of words, passed through my mind: time has played a trick on you. And almost simultaneously, Taylor's face appeared speaking its final words: 'You need me.'

I began walking home. How had time tricked me? The houses in Widlake Street had been transfigured by the green flames of the incendiaries, the white moon, the boarded windows. The street I had walked up two years before was repeating itself in a new, surreal key. It was as though time had curled back on itself and passed through the same location at one remove. Everything was in a new light.

When I eventually arrived back at my flat, I found it empty. Antonin Treiber had disappeared. Again – standing listening to the emptiness of my flat, the absence of the boy hanging in the air – I experienced that strangeness. Now it was as though the world were a train which I had missed, leaving me standing on a platform in nowhere.

IV

Questions

THE ONLY EVIDENCE that the boy had been in my flat was a couple of books that I noticed had been pulled from the shelf and left open on the floor amid my usual mess. I was about to replace them when I saw, by the seedy dawn light that was seeping through the room, an envelope lying on the doormat. It was from Aubrey Taylor. I opened it and found inside a poem.

THE FOUNDING OF CITIES

What tired liquid from these vessels,
What muscle-bound imaginings,
Can tell the story of this city?
Only in caves of fattened air,
The impressions of experience piled on experience
Are qualities of repetition.
This dug dirt. These crusted shells.
Are chastisements against excessive harkening.
The solidity of this town is undermined
By solitude, idleness, rats, drainage.
(In drawing rooms we know what passes;

We are etherized against our origins.)
For we must live on the crust of these streets. Break
That crust with bombs and you will find
The functions that serve our present needs:
Drainage, required transportation.
Yet it all began the other way round;
We even think of it as a natural growth.
And stories are there to be told.

There were a couple of others in a similarly drab vein, and with them a note asking me in an unctuous tone to spare a minute to glance at them. The tone and content of the letter were familiar to me, and only one phrase caught my eye: 'now that I can help you . . .'

Later that morning I phoned Peter Musgrave and asked if I could see him urgently. He was living for the duration in a flat close to the river in Pimlico. I arrived there on the dot of nine o'clock that evening. He had warned me on the phone that I could only have quarter of an hour because he had to 'get back to the House for a division'.

He was older than I remembered, with a well-oiled, chinless face beneath greying hair. I had held a grudging admiration for him back in 1938, when he had resigned the Conservative whip over Munich. Now he was being tipped for a job in Churchill's government. Greeting me, he moved with a diffidence that was not wholly upper-class affectation.

'I've come about Stefan and Antonin Treiber,' I said when we had sat down. 'I wondered if you had news of them.'

He betrayed no surprise, no emotion. 'To the best of my recollection,' he said, forming a steeple with his fingers and gazing at the ceiling, 'Stefan Treiber, the uncle, was interned in May of this year as a Category A alien. The boy was given Category B status and his movements placed under restrictions. As you may be aware, I have spoken in Parliament a number of times against the unnecessary internment and deportation of refugees from occupied Europe. Since the tragic sinking of the *Arandora Star* in July, when six hundred German and Italian deportees were killed, there has, I think, been a shift in the government's position. I believe we shall soon see the release of all aliens who do not pose a genuine threat to national security.'

'Did Antonin Treiber ever visit your house in Widlake Street?' I interrupted. I have always disliked being lectured by politicians.

'I believe he may have been there once, when a party of the Czechs were taken on a trip to the cinema in London. That must have been nearly two years ago.'

'Because I saw him there the night before last.'

For the first time, he looked straight at me. 'Impossible. The place has been locked and boarded up for months. My family are in Sussex.'

'He was in the basement of the house next door, with some squatters.'

There was a pause. Musgrave was staring at me. 'I don't understand.'

'I was hoping you might help explain it.'

'Do you mind if I ask what you were doing there?'

'I was with one of the squatters, a man called MacCready, a sculptor. We both drink at a pub nearby called the Belgravia Tavern. MacCready wanted me to talk to a foreign boy who had wandered into their basement. When I got to the place I found that this mysterious foreign boy was Antonin Treiber.'

'And what did Antonin Treiber have to say?'

'He didn't seem to have learnt any English. I gathered that he had been staying with a family somewhere outside London. I took him back to my flat to look after him and find out more about what he was doing there. But when I got back last night, he'd gone.'

This seemed to irritate him. He looked away, towards the

leather-bound volumes of Hansard in his bookcase. 'Well, I don't see what you expect me to do about it, Mr Morgan.' He didn't say it with any conviction.

'We were both responsible for the Treibers coming to England,' I said. 'Doesn't that makes us responsible for their welfare here?' I almost added, 'I know your type: very prepared to dole out charity when it suits you, but lazy about the long-term.'

'All I'm trying to discover, Mr Morgan, is what it is I can do in practical terms.' He looked at me as though to say, 'I know your type; the over-emotional Celt, long on words (and drink as well, probably) but short on practical action.'

The carriage clock on the mantelpiece chimed the quarter-hour, breaking the tension and reminding us both of Musgrave's 'division in the House'. He stood up and extended his hand. 'It seems to me that the best I can do is make some enquiries at the Home Office. If necessary, of course, we will have to inform the police. They may need your assistance. Ring me in a couple of days and I might have some news.' He ushered me out into the star-twinkling darkness of the blackout.

I hated Musgrave as I walked away from the flat. The worst part of it was that as far as the war went, Musgrave was on the side of the angels. He had opposed the government at Munich – and not just by sitting on his hands, but by actually resigning the Tory whip. Who could doubt that he would have 'a good war'? I rolled the loathsome phrase around my mouth. What about the millions, like Antonin Treiber, for whom there would be only misery? Wasn't it better to be drinking in the Belgravia with the likes of Taylor – out of sympathy, as it were – than having 'a good war'?

I descended into the Underground at Embankment. There were some hundred people – families, mostly – bedded down on the Northern Line platform. The parents played cards or talked among themselves, glancing up at the ordinary travellers who waited on the other side of the white line with a strange mixture of apology, hostility and suspicion. Their children were strewn about them in attitudes of helpless repose, heads back and arms flung out. How many of them would have 'a good war'?

And how many of the exhausted faces, rocked to and fro on the train, turning their ears against the clatter of the tracks, would have 'a good war'? I stared at my own face, a blurred white blob in the shuddering window opposite. Would I have 'a good war'? Just then, I couldn't face the prospect of going back to my flat, where the boy's disappearance would still be hanging in the air. I got off the train at Tottenham Court Road. There was still time for a late drink at the Belgravia.

I found Taylor at the bar waiting for me. 'MacCready was looking for you again,' he said.

Looking into his strange, pallid face with its ugly mixture of vulnerability and sullen defiance I had a sudden sensation of nausea, of being caught in a loop, the world spinning round and round like a fairground ride.

'Did you follow me last night, Taylor?' I blurted out a little wildly.

'Why should I?'

'You tell me. You send me your poems, you hang around me, you tell me I need your help. Why shouldn't you follow me?' As soon as I had said it, I felt ashamed of this outburst.

'You're beginning to imagine things, Morgan. That's all fear is, isn't it? Courage is just a failure of imagination.'

'What have I got to be scared of?'

'You tell me.' He gave me his thin-lipped smile.

'I'm going to find MacCready,' I said, annoyed by my own lack of control and by the look of sly satisfaction on Taylor's face.

Outside, I was sucked down the same tunnel as the previous night. I walked away from the pub. The pub door opened and closed behind me. I ran and fell. I lay heavily on my side, the night reeling above me. But this time I scrambled quickly to my feet and charged back in the direction I had come. A couple of seconds later, bending forward as if to make a rugby tackle, my shoulder banged into a woollen coat. The body inside it cried out and began to crumple. Then something hard hit the back of my head; something else thumped into my stomach. I began to be sick.

My dreams were filled with pain and with the imagery of Taylor's poems. A bright red worm, flashing in time to the pain, broke through the city's crust and burrowed down through the layers of pipes, cables and drains. At one point, as it ate its way down into the city, it fell through an Underground tunnel, twisting and turning through the air that was fattened and ripe with the exhalations of a hundred subterranean sleepers. It lay among the rails for a moment, sniffed at by a passing rat, before its jaws gripped the ground again. The scrape of tooth on concrete sent a ripple of wakefulness across the faces of the sleepers.

I woke. As if in response to the opening of my eyes, a policeman opened the door of the cell in which I was lying. I sat up and touched the tender bump on the back of my head. 'Is there a doctor?' I murmured.

'There's a war on is what there is,' he said. 'We've got better things to do than nursemaid every drunk who gets dragged in here. Get up.'

He led me down a long corridor. 'Is that what I'm here for?' I asked. 'Being drunk?' I was blinking in the brightly lit corridor. The policeman just jangled his keys. 'Are you letting me go now?'

He stopped, opened a door, and directed me through it to where another man, younger and dressed in a suit, was sitting at a table.

'Ah, sit down, Mr Morgan. I am Inspector Saville, Special Branch.'

I sat down at the table. My head was hurting.

'Name, please?'

'You just used it.'

'Name?'

'Henry Edward Morgan.'

'Age?'

'Forty-two.'

'Occupation?'

'I work at the Ministry of Information. Could you tell me . . .'

'Good.' The man flipped open a file and ran his finger down the first page. 'Have you been drinking this evening, Mr Morgan?'

'A bit.'

'Where?'

'The Belgravia Tavern.'

'Do you drink there often?'

'Quite often.'

'How do you know Antonin Treiber?'

I lifted my banging head. 'Where is he?' I asked. 'Is he here?'

'How do you know Antonin Treiber?'

'How do *you* know about him?'

'*How do you know Antonin Treiber?*' Without looking up from his papers, he spat each word out loudly, making my head hurt even more.

'I helped him and his uncle get out of Czechoslovakia in '38.'

'The uncle – what's his name?'

'Stefan Treiber.'

'Do you know him well?'

'No.'

'How well?'

'We met twice.'

'Good.' Saville looked up at me and smiled. 'Peter Musgrave. Do you know him well?'

'Not well.'

'When did you last see him?'

'I don't remember.'

'You're lying. You saw him this evening at,' he shuffled through the file and pulled out a piece of paper, 'nine o'clock. Is that correct?'

'Yes.'

'What did you talk about?'

'Antonin Treiber.'

'And what did you say about Antonin Treiber?'

'I told Musgrave that I'd seen him the night before last.'

'And why should that piece of information be of interest to Mr Musgrave?'

'Because Musgrave also helped Antonin Treiber and his uncle come to England.'

'And that is the extent of your and Mr Musgrave's interest in Antonin Treiber and his uncle?'

I nodded.

'And where is Antonin Treiber now?'

'I don't know. I took him back to my flat, but then he disappeared.'

'You didn't think to lock him in the flat?'

'Why should I? He's not a criminal.'

'So why did you take him back there?'

'I wanted to help him. I thought he might be in trouble.'

'But he didn't want your help.'

'Apparently not.'

'I don't believe you.'

'What don't you believe?'

'Almost everything. You've admitted lying to me once. Most immediately, I don't believe that you don't know where Antonin Treiber is.'

'Well, I don't. I want to find him. That's why I asked you – '

'Why do you want to find him?'

'I think he might be in some kind of trouble.'

'What kind of trouble?'

'I don't know.'

'So what makes you think he's in trouble?'

'You. All of this.' I waved a hand at the greyish pink walls of the interview room.

'You're lying again. You said earlier that you took him back to your flat because you thought he was in trouble. That was before you were brought here.' He smiled triumphantly and wrote something in his file. 'The uncle – where's he?' he continued without looking up.

'I don't know. He's been interned.'

'Did the boy say anything about him?'

'No.'

'What *did* the boy say?'

'Nothing.'

'I don't believe you.' He wrote in the file again. After a couple of minutes he looked up, as though surprised that I was still there. 'You can go now,' he said.

'I'm free?'

'Bugger off. Before I change my mind and charge you with assaulting an officer.'

I got up to leave.

'And by the way, Mr Morgan – '

I turned back in the doorway.

'None of this has happened.'

V

The Strawberry Sailor

I LAY LOW for the next few days, unable to summon the energy even to tidy away the wreckage of papers, books and plates of half-eaten food that covered the floor of my flat. I had phoned in sick to the office. The bump on the back of my head continued to give me blinding headaches, but these gradually eased. Then it was only lassitude and apathy that prevented me from rising from the sofa. Outside my flat, the bombing continued unabated.

I could not even bring myself to phone Peter Musgrave to gather what he had found out about Antonin Treiber. The bang on my head had dented my sense of mission. But when I returned to the office, after an absence of a week, I found a pile of messages from Musgrave on my desk, scribbled in different hands by whoever had happened to be passing when the phone rang. None of my colleagues had been aware of why I was not there, or had even particularly noticed my absence. The only person watching out for me, it seemed, was the man in a dark blue suit who had been waiting patiently in the street opposite my flat.

I hesitated a few hours before phoning Musgrave back,

extracting a small, childish pleasure from keeping him hanging on.

'Where the hell have you been?' he demanded. He sounded quite different.

'Ill. I fell down some stairs and banged my head.'

'You said you'd ring me back about this Treiber business.'

'What "business"? I just wanted to find out what's happened to the boy.'

'There's more to it than that. His uncle escaped from internment back in June. I got the details from the Home Office. Listen. "On the 28th of June, Stefan Treiber, along with fifty-seven other internees, was being transported by rail from Dover Court Holiday Camp, which was being used as a transit camp, to Ridge House transit camp in Bristol. The journey involved two changes, and the internees were guarded by a unit of military police under the command of Captain Brian Holden. On arrival at Ridge House it was discovered that Stefan Treiber, a Category A internee, was missing." Do you know what Treiber did before the war, Morgan?'

'He was in business.'

'Apparently one of his business interests was radio equipment.'

'I don't see what bearing that has.'

'Be sensible, Morgan. This is being investigated now by MI5 and Special Branch. I want to know what you've got me mixed up in.'

I felt a thrill of pleasure. Musgrave was scared.

'Are you sure you've got your facts straight?' I asked calmly. 'You're not imagining things? How could Stefan Treiber possibly escape from a train under armed guard? You've met him. He's an old man.'

'Dammit, man. I'm only telling you what the Home Office told me. As for how Treiber escaped, that's for the War Office to explain. They're in charge of security.'

'But why was he being moved to Bristol?'

'Ridge House was acting as a kind of sorting office. Some of them would be going on to the Isle of Man. Others were selected for deportation. All that happened at Ridge House.'

'A sorting office.'

'All that's beside the point. I want to know your part in this, and why you've mixed me up in it.'

I went on protesting my innocence, but Musgrave seemed convinced that he was the victim of some conspiracy. He was becoming more and more heated and unreasonable.

'Look here, Musgrave,' I said in the end. 'If you really want to discuss this further, I'll be in the Belgravia Tavern this evening. I can't talk any more now.' I put the phone down.

It was already late. In a state of some excitement, I left the office and walked several times around Russell Square, amid the silence of the streets and the dank smell of sodden upturned soil. Banks of sandbags partitioned the lawns. The only sound was the rumble and thump of distant anti-aircraft barrages. Somewhere out there, I thought, in the darkness, were Stefan and Antonin Treiber. A snail crunched under my foot as I turned towards Tottenham Court Road to make my rendezvous with Musgrave.

Behind its blackout, the Belgravia roared with drunkenness. The floor was sticky with beer that had slopped from the tables and counters. The air was thick with smoke and talk – endless talk, manic talk, talk as if talk were the only thing that could drag the dreaming drinkers from the pit they had dug for themselves. Everyone looked worse since the bombing had begun: shadow-lined eyes; yellow, sweaty pallors; expressions that twitched nervously as the drinkers strained to catch the drift of the conversations that swirled meaninglessly around the crowded room. What were they all doing here? The Belgravia was an exotic cyst on the surface of the silent, cowering city. In its state of emergency, with its empty streets and empty darkness, London seemed stretched to unbearable thinness, laid open to a sky that rained metal and explosions. But the Belgravia seemed to have imploded, to have gathered vast reserves of manic, nervous energy and hurled them into an ever-expanding inner space. Across that space the Belgravians made their internal migration. Drifting on an ocean of beer, blown by whiskies and gins, they were leaving the bombs far behind.

I skirted the groups clustered around the bar and found a quiet corner from where I could observe the whole pub. There were a few people I knew, but nobody looked in my direction. Perhaps, since I had been absent for a few days, they had entirely forgotten my existence. That would have been characteristic of the Belgravia.

Taylor was hanging about on the edge of a large group at the far end of the bar. I watched him straining to catch the conversation as it rattled past. His eyes darted from one face to another, and every now and then he threw in some comment, or laughed and shook his long head. But the people in front of him, who themselves were not at the heart of the group, had their backs half-turned to him. His interjections went unacknowledged.

The centre of attention in Taylor's group was Vivekananda, an Indian fellow who edited a poetry magazine and was definitely one of the Belgravia's bigger stars. Taylor had once shown him some of his poems and received a humiliating brush-off in return. Vivekananda was small, dapper and usually had a good-looking woman in tow. He had a couple with him tonight, which in itself would have guaranteed a good audience. Women were a scarce commodity in the Belgravia.

Vivekananda's cronies bantered on, drawing closer together. Gradually, Taylor found himself blocked out by a couple of broad, tweed-jacketed backs. I watched him bob up and down a couple of times, trying to join in, then attempt a nonchalant withdrawal. It would have been easy to pity this ridiculous performance, but I had no illusions about Taylor. Had he been inside Vivekananda's citadel, he would have been the first to pull up the drawbridge and leave some other poor sod out in the social cold. There was something unsavoury about his watchfulness and his air of cravenness mixed with sullen defiance.

He cast a last glance around the pub – I leaned to one side, putting a couple of drinkers between us – and retreated reluctantly in the direction of the door. He had just reached it, when it swung open and Musgrave entered. There was a moment of confusion as Taylor tried simultaneously to step out of the way and hold the door open for the newcomer. Then, suddenly, they appeared to recognize each other. I watched as Musgrave nodded and smiled a stiff smile. Taylor bowed and scraped. They swapped a few words – both rather awkward, Taylor unsure whether to close the door in order to continue the conversation. Then Musgrave extended his hand, excused himself and passed on. Taylor left the pub, glancing back one last time as he closed the door.

Musgrave bought himself a beer and came over to me.

'You know that chap who was just leaving?' I asked.

'Extraordinary thing ' he said. He reeked of spirits, which surprised me. I hadn't had him marked down as a drinker. 'Aubrey Taylor. Haven't seen him for thirty years. We were at school together. We used to call him the "strawberry sailor". Don't ask me what it meant. Something sexual, no doubt.'

'No doubt,' I said.

'Look here, Morgan, we've got to get to the bottom of this Treiber business. It's utterly outrageous that we should become the object of suspicions simply because we carried out a humanitarian gesture by assisting two refugees from Nazi-occupied Europe.'

It took him a while to negotiate his way to the end of this

sentence. I scrutinized him sceptically while he did it, sipping my beer. He was red-eyed and frightened. I was tempted to spurn his implicit offer of an alliance, to let him stew in his own juice. 'What makes you think we're under suspicion?' I said.

'I went to see Christopher Carlton today. He's a minister in the Home Office. We were at school together. He started interrogating me about Stefan Treiber and the boy. He wanted to know what the boy was doing hanging around Widlake Street.'

'How did Carlton know the boy had been there? Did you tell him?'

He stared at me with his blood-shot, scared eyes. 'I . . . I assumed you must have told them about it.'

'Well, I hadn't.'

'How did they know then?'

Stupid and scared, I thought, and shrugged my shoulders. Musgrave was silent for a few moments, lost in paranoia. 'I've never been so humiliated in all my life,' he began bitterly. 'Carlton and I have been, well, sort of friendly rivals ever since school. Senior debating society, the Union at Oxford, then in the Commons. We seem to have followed each other around the place. And now I find myself interrogated by him like some common criminal. I know what you're thinking, Morgan. You think I'm reverting to type. The pathetic public-school boy, obsessed with power, raised to it from the potty. Well, I don't give a bloody damn what you think. I just want you to come clean on what it is you're trying to mix me up in. Why the hell did you come and see me?'

It was clear to me by now that Musgrave had been drinking heavily, and that he wasn't used to drink. As well as the heavy-lidded eyes, the drooping head, there was his volatility. Within a few seconds he had switched from mateyness to rage. It was a long way from the mandarin calm he had displayed in Pimlico.

'So what did the Home Office tell you about Antonin Treiber?' I asked. It seemed best to stick to simple requests for information. 'That was why you originally went there, if you remember.'

'At the beginning of the war he was given Category B status by the tribunal on Czech refugees and lodged with a family in Guildford.' He had turned morose now. 'Respectable people. The father's a town councillor. The Treiber boy was to report to the police station every week. Anyway, a month ago he absconded. The family haven't seen him since. That no doubt accounts for his presence in London.'

'No doubt.'

'Well, it's a bit of a coincidence, you must admit, the uncle and the boy going missing at about the same time.'

'I wouldn't deny that, if it's true.'

'What the hell do you mean? I wish you'd stop talking in riddles, Morgan.'

'All I meant was, I'd be surprised if Stefan Treiber could slip past armed guards and escape from a train. And I still don't understand why he should want to.'

'I told you on the phone, one of his pre-war interests was in radio equipment.'

'What the hell does that prove? Nothing.'

'MI5 and Special Branch don't mount this kind of operation for nothing, you know. They have to have good reasons.' In another of his quick changes of mood, he had become pompous and indignant. 'If they decide to investigate Stefan Treiber, it's because they think he bloody well poses a threat to national security. And that has to come first.'

'Don't be ridiculous, Musgrave. The man's a Jew. He came here to escape from Hitler's mob. If he did escape from that train, which I very much doubt, I should think it was simply because he couldn't stand internment. I wouldn't be surprised if the poor bugger hasn't killed himself by now. That's more likely than him working for the Germans.'

'You don't know what you're talking about, Morgan. These are matters of which you have no knowledge.'

'Do you know what I think happened? It's just occurred to me. They killed him. He was dead when he came off that train, and now they're trying to cover it up by pretending he escaped. I don't know why I didn't think of it before.'

'For God's sake, Morgan, this is England.'

'No. Of course, you're right. If he really was dead, they wouldn't be bothering to have you and me watched.' I hadn't planned to say anything about that, but the childish, vindictive streak in me proved too much.

My remark had its effect. Musgrave's face sank, and he stared at me again with those bloodshot eyes. 'What do you mean, "watched"?' he said. 'Are you sure you're not bloody well imagining things again, Morgan?'

'Oh, I have a very limited imagination. But I know when someone hits me on the back of the head.' I told him what had happened, leaving nothing out. 'You'll notice,' I added when I'd finished, 'that nice Inspector Saville was particularly interested in my relationship with you, and that he knew the exact time of my visit to your flat. Now, I may not be an expert on these matters, but that sounds to me like we're being watched.'

'You mean *you*'re being watched. It's you that's being followed. I haven't done anything to justify being interrogated in the way that I was today. I resent the implication that I am associating with fifth columnists. It's you that's dragged me into this bloody business, Morgan.'

'I don't think it's so one-sided. How did they get on to me in the first place? What made them start following *me*? Do you know what I think? I think they've been watching your place in Widlake Street for a while – waiting for

Antonin Treiber, perhaps just watching for anyone who might go there. That's how they got on to me. So who's dragging who into things, Musgrave?'

Our eyes met, Musgrave's cloudy and confused.

'And another thing,' I said. 'Where is Antonin Treiber now? How did he disappear from my flat? I think they took him – your precious MI5 or Special Branch or whoever these men are. I think they kidnapped him and now they've killed him, or they're holding him somewhere.'

'You do too much thinking, Morgan. You're bloody mad.' Musgrave got uncertainly to his feet and peered down at me. 'You're a mad bloody Welshman.' He turned and staggered through the crowd to the door.

When he was gone, I laughed. I must have been quite drunk myself. I laughed and slapped the table. Tears filled my eyes, stung by the hot, smoke-filled air. Gradually my mirth subsided until I felt empty, ashamed, alone. The Belgravia was depressing me. I stood up and pushed through the crowd to the door. I was in the blackout, the moon clear above me. In the distance the bombers made a high-pitched rumble. I felt better. I began stumbling towards Widlake Street. I would visit MacCready. I had never got that snail from him. I was damned if I was going to give him nine-pence for nothing.

VI

Imagining Things

MacCready was alone in the basement. He sat at the table, one leg slung across the other, bending over a pipe-cleaner model which he was fashioning by candlelight. A hand-rolled cigarette smouldered in a jam-jar top.

'What the hell do you want?' he said, without looking up from the pipe-cleaners. 'Believe it or not, this is more than just a delightful joke to me. This is my living. But then you wouldn't understand that.'

'Spare me the violins,' I said. The walk seemed to have cleared my head. I was in a state of nervous exhilaration.

'Look at this.' MacCready took the candle and held it near his leg, to show where his trousers had split up the seam from knee to crotch. 'How would you like to walk around like that?'

'Sew it up.'

'Buy me a needle and thread.'

'All right. It'll be worth it not to hear you moaning on like this.'

MacCready shook his head and went back to fiddling with the pipe-cleaners. 'Do you know something, Morgan, I'm beginning to think these things have possibilities. I've got so many of the damn things, boxes and boxes of them back there,' he indicated the gloomy rear of the basement, 'that I was thinking of doing a proper sculpture, something big and solid-looking. If you wound enough of them together, curled them around each other so that they formed a kind of labyrinth, you could make it look solid. What do you think?'

'I can't imagine it. But then I never did have much of an imagination.'

'No. I don't suppose you did.' He worked away at the model, then added, 'What's happened to that boy? Is he still staying at your place?'

'He's disappeared. I don't know where he is now. In fact, that was something I wanted to ask you about. When you brought me back here that night and I recognized him, you said, "So you do know him?" '

'So what?'

'What did you mean?'

'I was just surprised that you seemed to know him.'

'If that was all there was to it, you'd have said, "So you know him?" But you said, "So you *do* know him?" What made you think I'd know him?'

'You've lost me now. It was probably just a slip of the tongue.' He pushed the finished model out into the middle of the table and surveyed it. A monkey was escaping up a tree, while below some snakes slithered around its trunk.

'You're a bad liar, MacCready.' I got up and walked across the basement, keeping my eyes on him.

'You know your trouble, Morgan? You have a devious mind. I did you a disservice just now: you have a particularly twisted, involuted imagination. And you're drunk.'

'Someone told you to bring me here, didn't they? That was why you thought I must know him. Tell me who it was. Tell me who told you to bring me here and I'll buy you a new pair of trousers.'

MacCready, smiling and shaking his head, pulled the model back towards him and made some minor adjustments by tightening the snakes closer around each other. 'I'm not going to be drawn into your English games.'

'I'm not English.'

'But you're playing their games now. I'm not involved. I'm just trying to survive.'

'Here.' I threw a ten-shilling note down on the table. 'Tell me. Who was it?'

MacCready looked at the money for a moment, then pocketed it. 'It was Aubrey Taylor.'

'Taylor? Did he give you money?'

He nodded, going back to his model.

'He gave you money and told you to bring me here to meet the Treiber boy?'

'That's right. It was the night before.'

I sat down again and stared at his hands working the pipe-cleaners. 'How did he know the boy was here?'

'I told you, I don't play these English games. He didn't give me a reason. He just gave me money.'

We sat in silence. My mind, jolted by what MacCready had just told me, was snatching at irrelevancies: things that I imagined myself for a moment to have known for a long time but could no longer hold; suspicions that shivered between clarity and absurdity. It was as though MacCready had pushed me off a great height. Things shot past and I grabbed at them.

The raid, which had come quite close while we were talking, seemed to have moved further off. I glanced at my watch and said, 'I must go.' Then I remembered. 'What about the snail I bought?'

'Since you didn't come back for it, I used the pipe-cleaners again for something else. It's a peacock now. I can't afford to waste any of those things. I'll make you another snail, if you insist.'

'I do. And another thing, MacCready: where *do* you get all the pipe-cleaners?'

'I buy them. They're practically giving them away. There's a war on, Morgan. You can't get pipe tobacco for love nor money. Who needs pipe-cleaners?'

I could imagine MacCready bending the pipe-cleaners around each other – matting them together with his fat fingers, making art out of detritus. I could imagine MacCready being drawn aside by Aubrey Taylor and given his task, notes changing hands across the beer slops and fag ends. And I could imagine, mind jumping and clutching, that unwanted exchange of words between Taylor and Musgrave. Taylor, of course, would not have known that Musgrave had come to the Belgravia to meet me – I hadn't been there for a week, after all, and the Belgravia had a short memory. So there would not have appeared to him to be any particular danger in greeting his 'old school friend'. But Musgrave knew the danger. He knew that I might be in there, watching. So now, in retrospect, the awkwardness of two acquaintances meeting after a long separation became something different. When Musgrave put out his hand, was it a cold, formal acknowledgement – or was it a gesture of impatience, as he hurried Taylor past him out of the pub? And when Taylor glanced back as the door closed behind him, was it to catch a last inquisitive glimpse of someone he hadn't seen for a long time? Or was it an attempt to discover the source of Musgrave's panic? Perhaps the same thought was dawning on him as the door swung to as had already occurred to Musgrave – that by seeing them together I might see the thread that linked them with MacCready. Taylor had paid MacCready to take me to the boy, to implicate me in what Musgrave chose to call 'the Treiber business'. Taylor was acting under orders from Musgrave, who had been playing with me all along, and who now coolly slipped me the line that Taylor was just an old schoolfriend whom he hadn't seen for years. As I walked away from Widlake Street this thread of thought, pulsing like something alive, wormed its way out of the drunken blackout and arranged itself tightly around my mind.

VII

The Snail

TOWARDS EVENING, A single cloud, as clear cut as a bleached bone against the blue sky, is splashed with red by the sinking sun. The people of the city, gabbling in their foreign tongue, hurry through the deepening shadows, while above them the sunset makes final preparations for the drama to come. Antonin Treiber understands the language of the air raid. The sirens' wailing spreads out over the rooftops like the cries of animals across a jungle canopy. The figures down below move quicker, hardly visible in the shadows that fill the street. There are no streetlights. All attention is upward. As the siren dies away, the pencil beams of the searchlights are already spreading out across the sky like a fan. Everything is quiet, expectant. The sky is a stage, the searchlights footlights.

There are more clouds now, but enough silver moonlight to illuminate the white lines painted along the edges of the road, the white rings that mark the occasional tree. He follows the lines. He walks down streets of small terraced houses. Everything is dwarfed by the vast empty stage above. Antonin is beginning to discover that if you scan the skies for a long time, your perceptions become inverted. The sky appears as a landscape spread out below you, while the earth becomes an airy, insubstantial thing from which you hang, like a bat. The city itself is soft and vulnerable, pinned naked to the roof of the world.

As he walks, Antonin sees fewer and fewer people. A man with a black helmet on his head, a white 'W' painted on it, hurries across the road and says something to him. He repeats it and points down the street. Antonin, as usual, smiles apologetically. The man makes a dismissive gesture and hurries on. The rumbling of the distant anti-aircraft batteries has begun. Nearer ones open up with loud, muffled thuds. From the open sky comes the upward drone of the bombers. The noise is so tense that it seems that the sky might suddenly snap and fly into fragments, like shrapnel. The city remains utterly still.

When the first bomb falls, Antonin stops and gazes upwards. There is a momentary break in the clouds above him and he glimpses the black shapes of the bombers high up against the silvery-blue glow of the moonlit night. He sees no bombs. But then there is a second explosion, nearer, and the sound of falling glass. A smell of damp earth steals through the solid darkness. As the explosion echoes down the deserted street, the darkness is broken by a light. A man rushes out of a doorway and stands looking up at the sky.

'They're back,' he shouts excitedly. 'They're back.'

'Get back in 'ere!' 'Shut the bloody door!' come other voices, and the man's arm is grabbed and he is dragged back inside. The door shuts.

Antonin runs towards the door through the darkness. Above and behind him there is the strangest noise, as though someone were scratching the air just above the rooftops with a fingernail. A moment passes, then an explosion shakes the ground. Antonin reaches the door, pushes it open, staggers in, and slams it shut behind him, leaning back against it to catch his breath. A dozen faces are staring at him. He is in a small pub, narrow, with smoky air and barely room enough for the few tiny tables alongside the bar. Cardboard has been tacked up over the windows. The faces stare at him with hard, suspicious looks. He smiles back apologetically.

'Well?' says the big woman behind the bar. It seems that the smile has offended her. 'What do you want to drink? This is a pub, you know. There's a shelter further down the street, basement of the church hall.' Antonin shrugs his shoulders and raises the palms of his hands.

'I said, THIS IS A PUB. SHELTER DOWN THE ROAD. What's the matter with him? He foreign or something?'

'Here, you don't reckon he's a Jerry pilot, do you?'

'Don't be soft, he'd have a uniform on.'

'Well, who is he then?'

Antonin looks from one speaker to another, smiling. His absurd helplessness seems to defuse the situation. A soldier gets to his feet and says, 'I'll buy him a drink.'

'You're drunk, Tommy.'

'Get me two bloody beers. I'm not scared of foreigners. There you go mate, get that down you.'

'He's probably got a transmitter under that coat.'

Another crump somewhere outside.

'There you go. He's giving them our position.'

'Chuck him out.'

'No. He's with me.'

'I'm going down to the cellar. You lot must be mad.'

'Go on, then.'

'What's happening?'

'Give us all another drink.'

'He's all nerves.'

'. . . another . . .'

'What's happening?'

But there are no more bombs. The small pub sinks back

into beery silence. The soldier who has rescued Antonin sits him down, treating him with solicitude. He does not seem drunk, but there is certainly something strange about him. He does not seem to notice that the boy understands nothing he says. The other drinkers have noted this fact, and exchange laughter at the soldier's expense. They think he is drunk.

He is in his thirties, with thick, wavy brown hair, a moustache and a soft face pitted in the cheeks with the scars of adolescent acne. If the beer has had any effect on him at all, it is to emphasize a natural gentleness. He speaks slowly, and so quietly that even his fellow countrymen find difficulty in following him. His slow, rambling monologues quickly lose them, and he often ends up talking to himself. He holds his left arm stiffly across his lap. Around his neck is tied a red handkerchief.

'I'm sorry I can't offer you a fag,' he says in a voice that is notably rounder than the working-class accents of the others in the pub. 'My last one. I have to make it last. I've got a theory, actually, based on Zeno's paradox. If you put a fag out between puffs, and make each puff smaller than the one before, then in theory you could make your fag last for ever. Intriguing idea, isn't it?' He smiles at Antonin, and Antonin, who has been glancing warily around the pub, meets his eyes and nods, because that is what he thinks he should do.

'Intriguing idea,' the soldier continues, 'Zeno's paradox. I read about that last winter in France. You'd be amazed how much time you get for reading in the army. All those hours lying on your back. Zeno's paradox. It drove some of the men crazy if they couldn't read or didn't like to. All winter, while I was reading about Zeno's paradox, we were building defences around Lille – tank traps, pill boxes. I must have laid a few dozen tons of concrete myself.' The soldier stops, staring at the table as though the memory of all that concrete has suddenly, physically, flashed up in his mind. Its effect is to produce a change of gear in his voice, so that when he continues, after a pause, it is even quieter and more halting than before.

'Tenth of May. Beginning of the worst three weeks of my life. Mind you, it was nice of them to let us get some food inside us before we had to move out. It was all right to begin with, like a Sunday drive. The Belgian border guards tried to stop us because we hadn't got the right papers. For a few hours we were conquerors. We only saw Jerry once. A couple of Messerschmitts flew over. Some of the blokes took pot shots at them, but they were flying too high. They were just having a look. There was a beautiful sunset that night. Flat countryside. Some time in the early hours we got to Louvain, on the River Dyle. It seemed like the whole of the BEF was dug in there already. Hundreds of blokes running around, trucks dashing here and there, shells exploding somewhere up ahead. Very lights. Yellow and blue. We knew we weren't far from the front, but they let us get a few hours' kip. Then we were moved up at dawn, and I got to work at my eighteen-pounder. We had a lovely camouflaged position on the edge of an old orchard, a lovely spot. It was a pity it wasn't autumn or we might have got some apples to keep us going.

'I hadn't even seen any Germans. Later, when I got back to Dunkirk, I saw these two young Scots lads who'd been in a bayonet charge. It had happened a few hours earlier, but they were still shaking. I don't mean just shivering a bit. I mean *shaking*.'

The soldier looks at Antonin, frowning. Antonin just nods, his eyes flickering around the pub.

'It was at the Albert Canal that things started to go wrong, because that's where we first withdrew. We were back on the road to Louvain. There was a full moon that night we moved back from the Albert Canal. Moonlight on flat countryside. Trucks, Bren-carriers, tanks rumbling along the road. Behind us, all the time, we could hear guns. Nobody'd told us where we were going. First light, we were carrying straight on through Louvain. Word must have got round about us pulling back, because civilian traffic started appearing on the road, carrying luggage, furniture, everything they could. Everyone was going in the same direction, trying to get away from the front. Maybe they were trying to get to France. And it wasn't just the civilians. When we got to Brussels we found half the Belgian army evacuating too. Those that weren't getting out were just standing by the side of the road, staring at us. They couldn't believe what was happening.

'There were jams five miles long getting out of Brussels. Everyone was getting jittery about parachutists and fifth columnists. Dog fights. Bombs, spent cartridges. It was warm, so everyone on the road's getting more tense. You don't want to sit in a traffic jam with the Luftwaffe overhead.'

It is still in the pub. The figures hunched at the tables stir now and then – raise a glass to lips or shift a bottom on the hard benches. But for the most part they are as frozen and monumental as figures in a Cezanne painting. Only the soft-faced soldier's lips continue to murmur into the cold air. 'They caught us near Tournai. It was at a crossroads and there was a travelling circus trying to get on to the main road. Three Messerschmitts came roaring down our necks and opened up with machine guns. They shot at everything – civilians, us, the circus. A couple of the elephants went mad. Bellowing like anything and then they broke loose and started charging around. There were people screaming and running out into the fields beside the road. A team of white horses galloping out across the fields with the girl who'd been leading them.

'That night we held a line at the Escaut Canal. Working

long shifts at the guns, not getting much sleep. More stories going around; most of the attack had come through the Ardennes hills, where they'd said they could never get through. The Maginot line had gone. I'd seen the *troupes de fortresse* on parade in Lille just a few weeks earlier, with badges saying *On ne passe pas* on their berets. Everywhere you'd hear that. The French soldiers, they'd slap you on the back: '*Tommee, ils ne passeront pas!*' And everywhere you went there were posters: *Nous vaincrons parce que nous sommes les plus forts*. It didn't come to much.

'People were saying the Germans had got to the Channel ports. We were cut off. Soon we'd be on half rations. Then we started pulling back again. We went right through those defences outside Lille. They were going to be abandoned. All that concrete for nothing. Zeno's paradox. We did a rearguard action after that. They set us up in a ruined castle. We were there for a day and a half, until Jerry started coming round the side of us and we had to get out. There was a moat in front of this old castle. Beyond that, there was a couple of fields and then a wood. The Germans were in the wood, sniping and shelling us. At night we'd send flares over to check they weren't sneaking up on us. There were some sheep and cattle in the fields between the moat and the wood, and they were getting caught in all the firing. One big old cow got it right in the leg and jumped into the moat. She was swimming round and round, bellowing with pain. It was worse than the shelling. I've always had a soft spot for animals. I had to crawl behind this low wall till I could get a good shot at her. It nearly got me killed.

'When we were pulled back from there, we were put on half rations. Everybody was short of sleep. The drivers would nod off when they stopped, and when the column was ready to move again the military police would have to come down the line banging their helmets with revolvers to wake them up. We were passing through places where the last war was fought. There weren't any trees higher than twelve foot. One night we were up on Vimy Ridge, where so many blokes copped it last time. We were watching the Germans take Arras. There was a glow across the country-side from two big fires, tracer shells across the sky, red and blue Very lights bursting. Every now and then a white rocket would go up, which was Jerry signalling their HQ they'd taken a new position. The next day our column got hit, a few got killed, and me and a few others got separated from our division. So we just started walking in the same direction as everybody else. Everyone was in shirtsleeves, and quite a few blokes had got themselves walking sticks. What with the heat and the blue sky, it was like a big weekend hike. Then the Stuka dive bombers would come back, or a couple of Messerschmitts would come down and machine gun the road.

'Everyone was heading in the same direction, for the Dun-kirk beaches. As you got nearer the coast, it got more and more crowded. Thousands of blokes moving in the same direction, and not much food around. They were killing everything in the farmyards. In the villages there were white sheets hanging out the windows ready for when the Germans got there.

'Near the coast it was all flat and open. No cover. The roads were up on embankments above the fields, a lot of dykes and canals choked up with the stuff that had been smashed up and dumped there. Everything that might help the enemy was smashed and thrown into the canals. A lot of burning too, especially trucks. Up ahead, to the left, we could see smoke and flames coming from the docks at Dunkirk. That was from fires started by the German bombs.

'We reached the coast somewhere between Dunkirk and La Panne. Hilly dunes with thick tufts of grass that could cut your hands, and beyond that miles and miles of grey beach. It was like the end of the world. There were thousands of men there, queuing up, wandering around, being sorted into groups. The dunes were full of men camped out. Whenever there was an attack, the men on the beach ran and took cover in the dunes. The evacuation had already started. Between raids there were small boats coming in, and a whole stream of men would wade out to meet them. It didn't look to me and the blokes I was with like we'd get a boat there in a hurry, so we started walking along the beach towards Dunkirk, where this column of black smoke was rising into the sky. We were hungry and thirsty by now. One of the men had gone bomb-happy. He was laughing all the time and dancing ahead of us down the beach. After a while we got to a big house on the sea front, turned out to be a hotel. It was all boarded up. Well, we broke in and looked around. There was no food and none of the taps worked. We had to drink water out of the cisterns. There were soft beds there and we lay down for a while. Then one of the blokes found a bottle of booze in the basement. I don't know what it was, but it was powerful stuff. Some kind of French spirit. We were taking turns to swig out of it and by the time it was finished we were rolling drunk. When we came out of the hotel on to the beach into the sunshine, it was like a holiday.

'Then all of a sudden these planes were screaming low over us, machine guns going and explosions. We were just standing there, smiling. I never did see any of those blokes again. The next thing I knew I was lying face down with my mouth and nose full of sand. My arm was aching. It'd probably have been worse if I hadn't been drunk as a lord. I rolled over, and all I could see were pools of blood soaking into the sand. Some of it was mine. I couldn't look at my arm. I think I was crying. Then I was on a stretcher. I was being carried along the mole at Dunkirk to a ship. The ship got hit and I was transferred to another. I think that was what happened. I don't know, I kept passing out. I remember seeing the water – it was just a lot of wreckage, oil, corpses. You could've walked on it. I felt a long way away from things by then. I was put in the hold of a ship with a lot of other wounded.

'But when we got back to Dover we were heroes. Cheering crowds, headlines in the papers. We all thought we were going to get shot for desertion. How could they turn *that* into a victory? I suppose because people know we're on our own now – just us and them. We haven't got to answer to the French or anyone. We know where we stand. The time came when Fat Boy Gort said, "We've had enough of this arsing about. We're going home." Like a snail getting back into its shell. Only some of the snail doesn't get back in quick enough, like at Dunkirk, and it's left there on the outside for the birds to peck at.'

The soldier gazes mesmerized into the distance, as though still seeing the beach. Antonin's sleepy, half-closed eyes watch the smoke from the soldier's forgotten cigarette curl upwards into the cold air of the pub.

VIII

The Thread

TWO WEEKS HAD passed since my conversation with Mac-Cready. The city was settling into its routine of nightly raids. A strange new life had emerged from the rubble of once-familiar landscapes; the bombs had shaken the kaleidoscope of the city into wholly unexpected patterns.

It was half-past eight, the sirens had sounded an hour before, and I was sitting in the living room of Musgrave's Pimlico flat. On the mantelpiece the carriage clock ticked quietly and beside it stood a forest of framed photographs – Musgrave's wife and three children; Musgrave at school and university; Musgrave with friends and political associates. Now I could see these emblems of Musgrave's life at a distance, as free-floating fragments snapped like dry twigs from another world, another time. I could see them for what they were. Now I could see Musgrave's performances – the mandarin calm, the drunken panic in the Belgravia – for what they were. Or rather, what they were not. For the effect of MacCready's revelation concerning how I had been set up – how my involvement in the 'Treiber business' had been arranged – had been to negate everything, as though

56

my experiences were written down and now had a line drawn through them, crossing them out. This image of a line through my experiences that served to say 'not this', 'this is not what was really meant' began to obsess me. I could see it, in a horrible, dizzying internal multiplication, itself crossed out – and that, and that. I had spent the next two weeks trying to track down Taylor, to confront him with what MacCready had told me. I had tried the Belgravia, of course, and I had visited the office at the BBC from which he was on 'sick leave'. I had found out his home address, and hung about on a depressing street corner beside a canal in Camden. The route that I traced in this fruitless hunt, going nowhere, bending back on itself, became involved, in my mind, with the line that MacCready had drawn through my experiences. For it was a line that not only negated everything, but connected it. 'You need me,' Taylor had told me one night in the Belgravia. 'Now that I can help you,' he had written in the note that accompanied his ghastly poems. That was perhaps the worst thing about the line, that it had been drawn in advance. It didn't so much trace my experiences as direct them. Taylor was drawing me down a tunnel whose twists and turns I had no choice but to follow. Everything was inside the tunnel. Things that spoke of 'outside' – those absurd photographs on Musgrave's mantelpiece, for instance – became just more dissociated fragments drifting through the fetid, closed-in air.

But don't think that I had lost my powers of independent thought or action. If I couldn't find Taylor, I could at least confront his paymaster. The line that MacCready and Taylor had drawn passed through Musgrave's drunken performance that night in the Belgravia. I had misjudged his powers of deception. I had misjudged everything's powers of deception. The quiet, measured voice that I could hear now through the open door of Musgrave's study had measured out its duplicity that night in doses of silliness, drunkenness and mock fear.

The telephone pinged next door and Musgrave came back in briskly, apologizing for the interruption. 'Now what can I do for you, Morgan?'

'I would have thought that was obvious,' I said.

'The Treiber business? I think we were both getting a bit over-excited about that. The best thing to do is to let the whole thing cool down and take its course. If the security services have investigations they must carry out, then let them do it. I don't think we should interfere in any way.'

'That wasn't the attitude you took last time we met.'

'I feel a bit embarrassed about that. As I say, I think we were getting a bit over-excited about that whole thing.'

How good an actor must you be to blush to order? How much calculation did it take to sham that spontaneous, foot-shuffling awkwardness? I looked at him steadily, silently – trying by my silence to intimate that I was seeing through him.

'Since we are both entirely innocent in this affair,' he said, sitting down in the armchair opposite me, 'we can have nothing to fear from whatever investigations are carried out. I should have grasped that essential truth before coming to see you that night. You must have thought I was behaving rather oddly.' He was smiling, but his right leg, slung over the left, swung rhythmically up and down. I watched it, wondering what this signified. Impatience? Nervousness? Or was this also something that I should doubt?

'Are we really both innocent?' I said, cleverly.

The leg stopped, and so did the smile. 'I did assume I was speaking for both of us. Is there something you want to tell me?'

'There's no need to pretend to be scared,' I said. 'We've had that. There's nothing I know that you don't. *I* know that now.'

'You're talking in riddles again, Morgan,' he said, and got to his feet.

I laughed. 'But of course, there *is* one thing you don't know that I know. Let's put all our cards on the table: I know about you and Taylor and MacCready. There – there's no need to pretend now.'

He made a gesture of impatience and walked away from me. 'Look here, Morgan, if you've been under some kind of strain, I quite understand. My advice is just to try and forget about this Treiber business. It's a difficult time for everyone.'

'Another one of your performances,' I said. 'Let me make it absolutely plain: MacCready has told me how Taylor paid him to take me to Widlake Street to meet the Treiber boy. Now you've got nothing to hide behind.'

'Taylor? You mean that chap Aubrey Taylor?'

'Yes, "that chap". Your "old schoolfriend".'

'But what's he got to do with it?'

Now it was my turn to get angrily to my feet. 'You think you can always find another lie to cover yourself with. But I'm not as gullible now as I was that night in the Belgravia.'

We stood facing each other for a few moments in silence. Then Musgrave said, in a different tone, 'I think I see. This chap MacCready told you that Aubrey Taylor had paid him to take you to meet the Treiber boy. You remembered seeing me greet Taylor in the Belgravia and jumped to the conclusion that I was involved in some kind of conspiracy with him.'

'Stop it,' I shouted. I stamped my foot, holding my head. 'For God's sake, stop it. How can you invent new lies, now? I've told you, I *know*.'

'This MacCready,' he began, 'are you sure he's being straight with you . . . ?'

I think I yelled something else at this point. I don't remember. Something made Musgrave back away slightly. 'Perhaps

you should talk to Aubrey Taylor,' he said. 'All I can tell
you is that I hadn't clapped eyes on him for about thirty
years before that moment.'

'I've been looking for him,' I said. I felt a bit calmer now.
'I can't find him anywhere. You'll see that from my point
of view there does seem to be a fairly implausible coincidence
here.'

'Perhaps.'

'And what does that mean?'

'It means that you should talk to Taylor. But if he tries
to implicate me in this thing, he's lying.' He moved towards
the door, and I found myself ushered into the darkness of
the blackout.

Somewhere below me the river slapped its banks. A hazy
moon lit a stretch of foreshore where ghostly gulls padded
silently up and down, flexing their wings. The rumble of a
distant barrage started up and at the same moment a gust of
wind whipped off the water, tugging at my hair. It seemed
possible, in this dreamscape, to believe more than two con-
tradictory things at once. MacCready could be lying. Musgrave could be lying. They both could be lying. Perhaps I
had been manipulated by Musgrave again – but I could no
longer care. I was a ball of string unravelling with terrifying
velocity. I strode on down the empty road, in search of
Taylor.

I passed the Houses of Parliament – Parliament Square
was deserted – and continued along the Victoria Embankment. There was a heavy raid going on out to the east. As
I rounded the bend of the river approaching Waterloo
Bridge, I could see the broad belly of the clouds beyond St
Paul's lit from below by massive fires. The dome stood out
faintly against the glow.

I crossed the bridge, went down into Waterloo Underground station and took the tube to Camden. The hills of
north London were stretched out below the moonlit sky like

soft, fleshy things. I went to Taylor's flat but found it dark and empty. I climbed Primrose Hill and sat looking out over the black city. In its night-shrouded, owl-hooting darkness, it could have been an eighteenth-century city, a seventeenth-century city. A black city.

I went down from the hill and retraced my steps to Taylor's flat. As I walked between the buildings – the tops of the buildings framing the dark, silver-blue sky, the whole world sucked up and overturned by that patch of dark blue sky – a machine-like swish rushed up behind me. When the bomb exploded I was lying face down in the road, and for the first time since the bombing had begun I was terrified. I ran, until I saw at a crossroads ahead a street shelter. It was of the type that people had told me was unsafe, with a flat concrete roof and flimsy brick walls. I ran to it anyway. ·

I slammed the door of the shelter shut behind me and leaned up against it to catch my breath. A group of twenty or more people looked gloomily up at me from the benches. I picked my way through to the only spare place, ducking under the bare light bulb that hung from the ceiling. A young child half-woke and began whining at its mother. The shelter settled, and the tired eyes of the shelterers wandered over me. I leaned my head back against the brick wall and willed my body to relax. My arm twitched, then my leg, as though strings had snapped inside them. I dreamed briefly of a vast forest and a column of night sky rising up above a forest track. I opened my eyes and saw the electric light slithering across the concrete. My fellow travellers hung their heads, sniffing at each other. Again there was a rumble and thud somewhere outside. I was about to close my eyes again, about to drift back down the forest track, when the door of the shelter swung open, and there was Aubrey Taylor. He stopped dead still in the doorway, staring back at me.

The other shelterers, sensing something strange, slowly

raised their heads and looked first at Taylor and then at me. Then the moment slowly unravelled. Taylor managed only the faintest of movements away from the door before I was stumbling over legs after him. I caught him about ten yards from the shelter with a rugby tackle from behind. He kicked and struggled, freed himself for a moment and began scrambling away. I caught him again and this time fell fully on top of him, hugging him in a close embrace. Taylor squirmed soundlessly, then was still. The shelter door slammed shut behind us.

We seemed to stay locked in that embrace for a long time. My mouth was close to Taylor's ear. I was about to ask him why he had set me up – I was about to drop that question into his waiting ear – when another shuddering bang jolted us from our dream. Taylor took advantage of my momentary relaxation to burst from my hold and scramble to his feet. Something thumped into my stomach and my brain was swamped with darkness. Inside that darkness, I knew that I had only dreamt the last couple of minutes and that I was still sitting in the shelter with my head resting back against the brick wall.

When I opened my eyes I was lying on the tarmac watching Taylor run away down the street towards the great glow from the east. I shouted after him, but whatever it was I shouted was lost in the boom of the anti-aircraft barrage starting up again. As I scrambled to my feet, I was gripped by a sense of theatre. I froze, crouched like a sprinter in my blocks. The guns and bombs rumbled around the dark tenements like thunderous applause around a vast stadium.

That hesitation was enough for Taylor to get away. I followed, but there was no sign of him. I wandered up and down the same streets, round and round, until I came out on to the broad sweep of a main road. Two cars, their hooded headlights carving out tiny arcs of light before them, crept down towards me. Then there were fire engines racing

along, bells clanging, their own hooded headlamps flashing
into the yawning entrance of an underground station. I
reached the station and stumbled down the stationary escalator.

There were hundreds of people sheltering there in the
labyrinth of halls, passages and platforms. They sat on steps,
lay in rows with children sprawled across them. At the
bottom of the escalator a small group of them were drinking.
They kept up a mindless, half-sung chant:

> *Old* Ribbon-drop, *Old* Ribbon-drop,
> *Cut* him up in little bits and *put* him in the pot!

One of them banged his bottle on the ground in time to it,
while the others waved their arms. Everyone else was gazing
apathetically at this group. Only one woman shouted at
them to shut up. It made me think again about Musgrave
and his 'good war'.

I moved further into the station. The air was fat with
smells, the light dim. The trains had stopped running and
down in the tunnel the shelterers had spread themselves to
the edge of the platform. A man's clear cough echoed down
the length of the platform and into the black maw at its end.
Looking down the long platform, over the huddled bodies
draped in coats and blankets, there appeared to be a light
mist in the air, as though the shelterers were giving off some
fine vapour.

About two-thirds of the way along, a man was standing
among the bodies in one of the weak pools of light cast by
the overhead lamps. He was looking along the platform, as
if unsure whether to proceed. In his uncertainty he glanced
back, and once again I found myself staring at Taylor. This
time we both moved instantly. I jumped off the platform
and started running towards him along the tracks. Taylor
stumbled through the shelterers for a few yards, dithered,

then jumped down on to the track himself and started running. In a few seconds he had disappeared into the blackness of the tunnel.

I stopped when I got to the entrance. The darkness in front of me was solid and soft. Behind me a murmur of surprised conversation had started up, then subsided. I peered ahead and said, 'Taylor, I know you're in there. You'd better come out now. There's nowhere else for you to go.' It didn't sound like my voice.

There was a long silence, and then, surprisingly close, a more familiar voice said, 'I'm here. I think I've done something to my foot.'

I still couldn't see him. Again I told him to come out, but all he'd say was 'I can't move it, I swear.' I edged forward to where the light thickened into darkness. Ahead of me was the great pit of the tunnel. I inched forward until I could make out Taylor's foot, his long leg, and then the rest of his body. He was on the ground beside the track, rocking backwards and forwards and cradling his ankle between his hands.

'I think I've twisted it,' he said. 'Look, I'll explain everything. I know why you're chasing after me and I can explain everything. MacCready told me that he'd told you.'

I stepped forward until I was standing threateningly over him. Now I could make out through the gloom his pendulous face. 'I hope you will be able to explain everything,' I said, 'including why you kicked me back there. But you can start with who you work for. MI5? The police? The Germans?'

'It's nothing like that.' He winced with pain.

'But you admit that you paid MacCready to take me to the boy?'

'You've got to help me, Morgan. This ankle's killing me.'

'When you've told me.'

'All right, all right . . . I was sent to school . . . I was seven years old . . . to prep school . . . then public school, a place out in the country . . . there was a group of boys in my house . . .'

'And one of them was called Peter Musgrave,' I interrupted, 'and you ended up working together, with you running dirty errands for him. I know this story.'

'No . . . Musgrave was never part of it,' Taylor continued in his strange way, rocking backwards and forwards with his eyes closed, speaking in painful bursts. '. . . he was a teacher's boy . . . he never liked games, our kind of games. He played rugger, cricket, but he never liked our games, real games, the kind where you make the rules up as you go along, impose *your* rules on the other players. Musgrave would never play that kind of game . . . always wanted the teacher's rules . . . he thought we were strange – that was why he hated Christopher Carlton, because he wouldn't play by the teacher's rules. But I loved Carlton. I could only make up stupid stories, that nobody wanted to read, but Carlton could make things happen. He told stories with people instead of words. I loved him, but I've never trusted him – he'd have hated that. He told me never to trust anyone, least of all him.

'At night our group gathered in the junior dorm toilets and we talked about the other boys – their weaknesses, their strengths – and in talking about their weaknesses and strengths to each other we revealed our own. Or thought we did. When a weakness was out in the open, it could be seized on, and pressed and pummelled and used, and that boy could be destroyed.

'Carlton was good at that. He made things happen. He made *us* happen . . .'

Taylor opened his eyes and looked up at me with unpleasant intensity. I felt myself shrinking away from him, away from the oppressive darkness of the tunnel.

'Why do you think men like lies?' he continued. 'I'll tell

you: because they like things twisted. It's all lies, what poets say about beauty and truth; what we like is twisted things. Let me show you something. Take this paper – never mind what's on the other side, save that for later. Now take this pencil and draw on it. Close your eyes, just let your hand move the pencil automatically. Now, look at what you've drawn. It's a spiral, isn't it? You see, that's what's inside us, something forever twisted. Something involved, spiralling inward to infinity, like waves rolling in on themselves before they ever reach the shore. And it was the snake that first sold us pleasure – twisted pleasure.'

'I don't give a damn about your party tricks,' I interrupted. My voice echoed closely around the tunnel. 'You're going to be straight with me. Why did you pay MacCready to take me to Antonin Treiber?'

'Isn't it obvious by now? Carlton told me to. I did it without asking why. I've always done anything for Carlton. I wanted to be in his story.

'Of course, I had my theories as to why. I knew that MacCready was living next to Musgrave's place, and Carlton has always hated Musgrave. Perhaps this boy with the foreign name was a spy. Perhaps Carlton wanted to link that name with Musgrave's. Then I saw you talking to Musgrave that night in the Belgravia. You became the link. It was wonderful, just like those midnight intrigues in the toilets. And when MacCready said that he'd told you about me, I knew that you'd be after me, dragging your lack of subtlety along behind you like a caveman's club.'

'So why are you telling me all about your old friend Carlton now?' I said. 'That's hardly very loyal. Or is it just my caveman's club making you talk?'

'How can you be disloyal where there's no trust? Carlton doesn't trust me, or anyone, except himself. He will already have imagined this conversation. I told you, he is making *us* happen.'

Again he looked up at me in that peculiarly intense way, and I said, 'What do you mean, "us"?'

'Why do you think you've been chasing after me? You need me.'

He stretched out his arms to me from the darkness of the tunnel. I turned and walked quickly back into the light and the fetid air of the crowded station platform.

IX

Spirals

LIKE A BAD dream, the next night found me back in the Belgravia. Taylor and MacCready loomed out of the crowd. The place had become reduced to these two grotesque faces – one gross and bluntly aggressive, the other angularly mean – leering out at me. The three of us went to the bar and started drinking.

Taylor said nothing about our encounter the previous evening. He watched me observe the bandage on his foot, the walking stick he was carrying. He smiled obsequiously. But I could tell immediately – from the way that his glance flicked away and rested on MacCready – that he had transferred that manic attention that had engulfed me in bad poetry. When I turned and walked away from him in the tunnel, it had snapped something. The eye of his obsession had moved on.

MacCready was setting out his stall on the bar, a long line of pipe-cleaner animals. There were familiar ones – the monkey swinging from the tree, the elephant, the giraffe. But there were new ones as well, though these had been done in such an abstract style that it was difficult to make out what they represented. There was certainly a rhinoceros, and something that looked like a bull or a buffalo. Somehow, from the spindly pipe-cleaners, MacCready had managed to impart mass and movement to the beasts. As the evening wore on, the beer swilling round and round in my head, I found myself staring at them so hard that I could hear the thundering of their hoofs, see and smell the dust that filled the air around the beer mats and ashtrays.

I had early on picked out from this stampede the snail that rightfully belonged to me. I kept it close to my elbow, and as the sealed-off world of the Belgravia bubbled about me, I looked down at its spiralling patterns more and more. The drink was making me bellicose and paranoid.

'So what's going on between you two?' I demanded eventually, glaring at MacCready and Taylor. 'This,' I continued, holding up the snail by way of explanation, 'and your little party trick last night, Taylor? Are you both trying to drive me off the rails? Well you won't do it. I know precisely what you're up to. You tried it with the Treiber business and I saw through that. It won't work.'

At first they pretended not to understand what I was talking about, so I explained to MacCready how Taylor had got me to draw spirals like the ones in the model of the snail. I fetched the crumpled piece of paper out of my pocket to show him. Taylor seemed delighted at the idea that he was involved in some kind of conspiracy with MacCready. MacCready was less impressed.

'Automatism?' he sneered in his Scots accent. 'The spiral was the kind of thing you stopped being impressed with your first week in art college. The most primitive kind of ornament. Leonardo used it a lot, of course, for human hair, swirling water, plant forms.'

'What about this then?' I demanded truculently, holding up the snail.

'I wanted to do a snail, not a spiral. It happens that snails involve spirals. Besides, Morgan, you didn't have to choose it. You could have chosen any of them. Why don't you buy another one, if you're unhappy with the one you've got?'

He turned away to talk to a couple of men in khaki who were admiring the animals. I spent the rest of the evening insulting Taylor and watching that non-existent stampede along the bar of the Belgravia. At chucking out time I was so sozzled that it took me three hours to find my way home through the blackout. I woke up fully dressed on my bed. In my hand I had the piece of paper on which Taylor had got me to draw spirals. I must have read the poem on the other side before falling asleep, because, reading it again, I was irritated by how precisely it described my own bleak dreams. This one didn't have a title:

> Large animals walk across my mind.
> Yet not yet. I know their kind,
> The kind of bulk that breeds all forms
> And stands back to view the shore
> In unhurried red colours –
> Eyes on woman and boy tell us:
> They stand parted by paint that cloys,
> In erect motion. A fixed poise.
> The sea has gone from their eyes, withdrawn
> Across a blasted bed that is dry and torn.
> Landscape ever more serious to the touch, till
> Snailsucked to the flatness away from the hill
> She stands upon. A reason exists
> To walk on this earth as hard as fists.
> It is to bring the sea back home.
> It is to bring the sea back home.
> Far away a wall of water
> Grinds the ground: harder, tauter,
> Nearer. Danger grips a sky,
> Purple winds etched by sight.

The Snail

Turn slowly back to shore
And walk, leaden; cry some more.
No way out of a pillar of air.
The solid circle of sea: 'Dare
To make your move!' Try:
Not too hard, not tonight.

I was beginning to see spirals everywhere. Sitting on the
bus to work, gazing at the crowds which gawped from
behind lines of white tape at a bombed-out shop, I began to
notice the smoke from my cigarette rising in a single line to
begin with, then widening into a bluish sheet, thick at each
end, before breaking into always moving but precise swirls
like the ones I had drawn – like the ones in MacCready's
snail. And at lunchtimes, feeling tired and hungover, I
walked down to Great Russell Street and sat beside banks of
sandbags on the steps of the British Museum. I would just
begin to feel better, gazing up at the clouds streaming across
the sky, when I would notice the scrolls high up at the top
of the doric columns. It gave me an unpleasant feeling to
look into these spirals, but once I had noticed them I couldn't
remove my gaze. It was difficult, but a relief, to drag myself
away from the steps of the British Museum and back to
work.

Getting to see Christopher Carlton was hard. Flunkeys
fobbed me off and when I did at last get through to 'the
minister', he sounded harassed and impatient. In the end, he
agreed to meet me at his club for tea. I refused to tell him
what it was about. Carlton was no more than a name to me
and I had no intention of involving myself in the intrigues
of a couple of politicians. But I was determined to get to the
bottom of what had happened to Stefan and Antonin Treiber. The more I thought about it – and I thought about it
all the time – the more the whole business seemed to be a
conspiracy hatched by Carlton to discredit Musgrave. The

story that Stefan Treiber had escaped internment (and was thus a potential spy) would serve that purpose, since Musgrave had sponsored his immigration. And linking Musgrave to the nephew – through myself and through Antonin's presence in Widlake Street – could only reinforce the impression that Musgrave was engaged in potentially treasonable activities with the Treibers. It was rubbish, of course, but it was the kind of rubbish that those responsible for national security liked to believe. And almost anything could be believed in the name of national security.

From Taylor's outpourings, I had been expecting Carlton to be a magus, a smooth Machiavellian monster with greased black hair, ice-blue eyes and a winning smile. In fact he was a gloomy-looking chap, running to fat, with a thatch of thick blond hair. He motioned me to sit down and listened intently while I held forth. I had planned my opening attack meticulously in advance. I told him how MacCready had taken me to meet Antonin Treiber in the basement and how the boy had disappeared from my flat. I told him how I had consulted Musgrave and how I had been followed and interrogated. He showed no reaction to my narrative. I told him about Musgrave's discovery that Stefan Treiber had 'escaped' from internment and about my discovery that my meeting with Antonin had been arranged. The climax of my story was Taylor's claim that Carlton had ordered him to set up that meeting. I had been expecting an angry or scornfully dismissive denial at this point. I paused, but none came. So, on a self-righteous note, I continued:

'Now, Mr Carlton, I object to being used in this way. No one wants to be a pawn in somebody else's game. But I can look after myself. What I object to more is the use of innocent and helpless refugees for the purposes of sordid political manoeuvring. I know why you told Taylor to set me up. It was because you wanted to fabricate evidence that Peter Musgrave still had some kind of connection with the Treiber family. Evidence would then be fabricated that the Treibers were engaged in spying activities and, hey presto, the end of Peter Musgrave. You wanted that because you had a hatred for Musgrave that went back to your schooldays, and because Musgrave had been asking embarrassing questions about the government's treatment of aliens and refugees. As a junior minister in the Home Office, you had an important part to play in those policies and by discrediting one of your principal critics you could smear the whole movement of opposition to government policy on internment and refugees. Now, I don't give a damn about your private battles with Musgrave, or even about the government's internment policy. But I do care about Stefan and Antonin Treiber. I'm giving you a choice. Either you tell me what has *really* happened to those two or I'm going to hand this whole thing over to my friends in the Press. I simply don't believe that Stefan Treiber could have escaped from internment or that he could be any kind of spy. He's an old man, physically and psychologically weak. As for the boy – he's sixteen and barely speaks a word of English. I want to know where he is now. I don't believe he'd just disappear like that for a second time.'

Carlton frowned, stirring his tea slowly, but didn't look particularly impressed by my threat. We both knew that no journalist would publish that story, standing as it did on the shaky grounds of conjecture and Taylor's testimony. Taylor was not a convincing witness. And besides, the story was unpatriotic.

'I think you've been paying rather too much attention to Aubrey Taylor,' said Carlton. 'It's true that I was at school with him, and a very rum customer he was, too. To put it at its kindest, he has a powerful imagination. Or you could say he was living in a world of his own. He has an obsessive character. He latches on to people and develops fantasies about them. Perhaps he's latched on to you in the same way?

For years he's dogged me, but it's hard to shake him off without being cruel. People like that imagine some special, mysterious bond. Taylor's been telling me that for years. He likes to pretend that he's my disciple. God knows what it is I'm meant to be teaching him.'

He looked at me with a pained expression, as though he found it hard to be so frank. I didn't know how to respond. Perhaps I've always been ambivalent about those in authority – suspicious, but always wanting to see their human side. A soft touch, only with sullen resentment under the surface. A bit like Taylor, in fact. What Carlton had just told me was so close to my own experience of Taylor that I just nodded, immediately believing in his point of view.

'However,' he continued, 'I'm glad you've brought my attention to this case. In view of what you've said about Stefan Treiber and the boy, I'll look into exactly what is going on and what enquiries are being pursued. I hope you'll bear with us.'

So that was that. He handed me a plate of scones and I noticed with a queasy feeling that the tiny butter pats were curled into elegant spirals.

X

The Sea

FIRE ENGINES SWISHING over broken glass make a sound like the tide tugging at a shingly beach. The sunlight glitters on neat piles of it in the gutters. Two young women come up to the soldier and say, 'Where are we?' They hold their smart coats tight around their chests, and have an urgent look in their eyes. The soldier stops – the boy at his side stops too – and they look around at the acres of rubble. Scraps of smoke drift skywards. Here and there a house is still standing. The soldier looks around, scratches his head and laughs and says that he thinks that that's such-and-such street and so this must be so-and-so. But it all looks different now. One of the women laughs loudly and says, yes it does look different. And they all stand there in the street and look around. There is more light here than they are used to, as though they had just come out of a thick forest into a clearing. Their eyes measure out the unexpected gaps and flatnesses of this new world. Wouldn't think it was all so flimsy, says one of the women, the one who had laughed, and the soldier says, why don't you two come along with us, we're going to see if we can't get a cup of tea around here? That would be nice, says the woman, and the four of them walk up the street in the direction from which the women had just come.

The glass even glitters like water. Looking at it, Antonin is thinking again about the first time he saw the sea – saw it properly, that is, for the boat journey across the Channel had been at night, when the sea was no more than a dark movement that rocked the tiny cabin he shared with his uncle. And when they landed at Dover, delivered to crowds and bright lights, it was no more than an unfamiliar, sour stench and – during a lull in the commotion – the sound of slapping water against the dockside. But, two weeks after his arrival in England, he really saw the sea. He and his uncle were taken on a trip to the coast by a rich Jew from London, a man with whom Antonin's uncle had done business many years before. During the short journey, the man tried to get Antonin's uncle talking about the old days when they had done deals together. But Stefan would only raise his eyebrows in mild acknowledgement of what the man had said, then turn to look out of the car window at the famous English countryside. The man preferred talking in English, so Antonin only learnt what it was he was saying later, from his uncle. He was telling them that England was the best place in the world, that England was the most tolerant place in the world and that they had done the best possible thing (he himself had done it ten years before) by getting out of Europe and coming to England. This, of course, was the last thing that Antonin and his uncle wanted to hear, because they were worrying about the rest of their family, Antonin's parents, who were left behind.

In the late afternoon the sun had glittered on the English Channel. The man from London stopped the car at the top of a cliff and started reading his newspaper. Antonin and his uncle were released, to breathe the sea air. Stefan rested on a bench, while Antonin walked on down the broad hill. The sea seemed to stretch away forever. It was exactly as he had imagined it to be from films and photographs, only more so. He had never seen so much sky. He walked on, over another hill, until he was out of sight of his uncle and of the car belonging to the Jew from London. He stopped and stared at the sea for a long time. He didn't know whether you could see France from here. At some moments there appeared to be a dark line that must be France; but at other moments it seemed to be no more than the horizon, where the curve of the world met the sky. One moment Antonin stared at the line and imagined France – a cliff like this, perhaps – then straight beyond that Germany, and beyond that landlocked Czechoslovakia, and Prague, and his mother and father. And at the next he would imagine the great curve of the world and try to picture how Prague lay on that round world in relation to himself now. Flat or curved, Antonin thought about nothing but this separation. Again and again he measured out in his mind each yard of sea and land that kept him from his parents. All his old battles and resentments against them had faded away, leaving only a yawning need that felt as wide and empty to him as the English Channel itself.

The afternoon drew on into evening and still Antonin remained at the top of the cliff. From time to time he crouched down and his eyes filled with desperate tears, and then he would stand up again and look out across the Channel as though he had just seen something coming over the horizon. Away to his right, over the land, streaks of low cloud etched red into the sky. The tide was out, sucked away from the cliff to reveal sand and mud and rocks. Antonin imagined himself down there on the flat sand, among the rocks, looking up at himself, at the figure standing on top of the English cliff. The figure on the cliff became his mother, so far away from him that she was a fixed, motionless thing, just a point of focus in a landscape. Everything whirled around Antonin and he felt himself rooted in the mud, staring up at that unreachable statue on the cliff. The sea had been blasted away from him by an ancient, slow violence.

He turned and began walking back towards the car. Ahead of him the sunset had contracted, glowing more fiercely as it sucked all the radiance from the sky into itself. It reminded Antonin of a piece of music he had heard, with his parents, at a concert in Prague. It had been a long and tempestuous piece, ending quietly, intensely, with long notes on the violas. These notes had glowed fiercely, as though the passion of what had gone before was growing more concentrated as it moved further and further away.

When Antonin got back to the car, the man from London berated him in Czech for being gone so long. Didn't the boy know that he had an important engagement in London that night? Antonin, in tears, shouted back that if the man was so busy then he shouldn't have bothered bringing them down here. Did he think that he and his uncle were beggars or paupers that needed charity? And why could he not talk Czech with them, instead of speaking all the time in English? The man told Antonin that he was an insolent and ungrateful boy, and that he would have been ashamed to have had a son like him. Stefan just looked away, smiling sadly. They drove in silence back to the big country house where Antonin and Stefan were staying.

There were many other Czechs staying at this house, but the atmosphere was cold and unfriendly. Everybody was suspicious of each other, distrustful of each other's past and of their motives for coming to England now. Some of them were socialist politicians with their families, and to them Stefan Treiber was just an old Jewish capitalist. Antonin, if they noticed him at all, was by association just a young Jewish capitalist. Everybody spent their days writing letters, filling in official forms, attending English classes, being interviewed by government officials and welfare organizations. All this activity passed Antonin and his uncle by. Antonin had made a decision at the beginning not to attend the English classes. He hated England and its people, and was damned if he was going to learn their gobbledegook language. All he wanted to do was go home. When he told his uncle this, Stefan nodded understandingly. He didn't make Antonin go to the classes. He didn't make Antonin do anything.

They spent the evenings in their room, playing chess or chatting aimlessly about home. They never ventured into the common rooms. During the day Antonin wandered around the grounds of the house trying to avoid the gardeners, who always found a reason to shout at him. None of the servants at the house were friendly to the foreigners, since they resented having forty Czechoslovakians dumped on them by their absent master. But gradually, as they found jobs and places to live, the refugees trickled away from the house. Only Antonin and his uncle were left. They were visited periodically by officials of charity organizations, who would interview Stefan and leave again exasperated. There seemed to be nothing that could be done for this old man and for his nephew who refused to learn a word of English. They were living in a strange limbo, imprisoned by oak pannelling and looked down on by gloomy English ancestral portraits. Stefan read English novels from the library, while Antonin, who had discovered a box of artist's materials in one of the attics, took up drawing. He would sit out in the weed-infested rose garden for hour after hour, making painstaking copies of plant forms.

When the war broke out they had to leave because the family of the man who owned the house was returning to claim their home. Antonin, remembering the night at the cinema, hoped that he and his uncle might be sent to London, but in the event they found themselves in a hostel run by one of the charities in a small town in the Midlands. Antonin was given an apprenticeship as a mechanic, but as he could still speak no English, he was left by himself in the corner of the workshop to fiddle with an old motorcycle engine. He spent the days gazing out of the window at the rain drizzling on to the rooftops. Then, in early summer, came catastrophe. Some men came and took Stefan away. Stefan told his nephew that he thought he was being taken to a kind of prison, but that he was sure everything would be fine. Antonin tried to get an address from him that he could write to, but his uncle was very vague and just smiled in that sad way of his. They took Stefan away and a couple of days later Antonin was taken away too, to the family of bullying father, cold mother and smirking children.

Mugs of tea and corned-beef sandwiches are being handed out from the back of a van. The soldier queues up and takes some to Antonin, who is sitting on the kerb, staring into a pile of broken glass. The two women have drifted on in the direction that most of the crowd are moving. Office workers – men in suits carrying umbrellas, secretaries with attaché cases – pick their way over the rubble. A group of brown-uniformed pioneer corps men stand by a bombed building, awaiting orders and eyeing the secretaries. When he has eaten, Antonin picks up a piece of glass and begins scratching with it on the kerbstone. He has not drawn since leaving the big house. He looks around for something to copy, but there is nothing here that he finds attractive, so he closes his eyes and copies what he sees inside his head.

The soldier and the boy wander around the city together all day. They find a place where soup and bread are being handed out. They stand behind lines of white tape and watch the pioneer corps work on a block of flats that has collapsed. The grey-uniformed ARP men stand around importantly. Last night was a big raid, and by afternoon today there are queues forming outside the Underground stations. Antonin has been down there before and likes the feeling of many people pressed in together. It reminds him of the cinema – the warmth, the darkness, the ghostly light on so many faces. He likes being in a crowd. It was the aloneness that drove him from the flat where the fat man had taken him. In the afternoon, when everything was quiet, he had just walked back out into the city.

It is mostly women and children in the queue, and the soldier is strangely docile and passive. Occasionally he will launch into a muttered monologue, but much of the time he is silent and seems helpless. Antonin feels like the responsible one. They wait in the queue for a long time, and Antonin passes the time by drawing on the outside wall of the station with his piece of glass.

In the late afternoon they are let in. There is a lot of shouting and laughter as they go down and stake their claims to places along the platforms and in the corridors. There are some arguments as late-comers muscle in and take places on the stairs, forcing those further down to crowd up. The trains still pull in and out and the passengers pick their way past the shelterers like the secretaries picking their way over the rubble.

The soldier sleeps early, turning and mumbling a lot. Antonin, sitting with his back to the tunnel, is still awake. He looks down the length of the platform at the shelterers bedding down for the night. The trains stop. The air is gradually filled with sleep, like a gas that can be smelt and tasted. It rolls down the tunnel in great waves, breaking momentarily on Antonin. In the instant that it breaks on him, Antonin is back on the night boat across the Channel, with the invisible sea rocking him and his uncle to and fro in their tiny cabin. Then the wave of sleep washes past him, and he is awake again and looking down the rows of shelterers, whose blank-lidded faces gaze into the dim lights.

There is now a vast ocean of sleep in the tunnel, an ocean of dreams and visions. It eddies and splutters as the shelterers snore and snort. All the time it rocks them back and forth.

Hours later, Antonin feels restless and oppressed by the narcotic atmosphere in the tunnel. He gets up and makes his way along the platform, through the corridors and up the stairs towards the surface. The metal grille across the entrance to the station is partially open. He steps out on to the empty road, breathing the cool, moonlit air. The drawings he had been doing while they were queuing to go down are on the wall beside the entrance. He takes the piece of glass from his pocket and starts adding to them, embellishing them. His mind is still cloudy and lulled from the atmosphere of the tunnel.

A light flashes in his face. A man with a torch is coming towards him down the pavement, saying something to him. The man is joined by another. Antonin stands up – he has been crouching to draw on the wall – and stares at them. When they are near, he drops his piece of glass and runs as fast as he can in the opposite direction. The darkness swallows him instantly.

XI

A Typing Error

I HAD NOT expected to hear from Carlton again. In retrospect it seemed that I had been fobbed off. My threat to go to the Press – if it had ever been serious – had evaporated. I phoned Musgrave and told him about Taylor's revelation and my inconclusive meeting with Carlton. He refused to meet, saying that all his time was taken up 'in the House'. He affected an air of insouciance, as though I were making a fuss over nothing. He was trying to distance himself. But this didn't bother me – I was concerned with the Treibers, not with Peter Musgrave.

Then, a couple of weeks later, I realized that I was no longer being followed. The figures in the shadows near my flat and under the trees in Russell Square had disappeared. It was as though they had never been there. And about a week after that Carlton rang me.

The following day found me sitting once more in Carlton's club, among the curled butter pats and fake doric columns. After some bland talk about the latest raids, the conversation came round to the Treiber business.

'I'm afraid I have some bad news,' he said. 'There's been

the most awful series of blunders. It now transpires that Stefan Treiber is dead. I'm instituting a full enquiry into how it all could have happened.'

I gazed at the butter pats, trying to turn this news over in my mind. 'How all what could have happened?' I said.

'It turns out,' he began in his pained manner, 'that Stefan Treiber was aboard the *Arandora Star*, the ship carrying deportees to Canada that was hit by a torpedo in July. He shouldn't even have been on it. It was only intended that German and Italian aliens be deported. It seems that there was the most frightful cock-up at the Ridge House transit camp in Bristol. They were sorting out the internees, picking the Category A German and Italians for deportation and sending the rest to the Isle of Man. It seems that the confusion arose because at Ridge House Treiber answered questions in German. They assumed he must be a man called Simon Treidel, a German who was in fact due in the next train load. It seems that Treiber just went along with this, if indeed he knew what was happening at all. So he was packed off to Liverpool. Then it was discovered that Stefan Treiber hadn't turned up and they assumed that he'd jumped the train.'

'But what about when the real Simon Treidel turned up in Bristol?' I asked. 'Didn't they realize their mistake then?'

Carlton shook his bowed head. 'The whole thing is quite unforgivable. They didn't, because by then they'd already sent the relevant files off to us at the Home Office. There were different officers on duty, who didn't know that one Simon Treidel had already been through the system. I'm afraid the awful irony is that the second Simon Treidel, the real one, was also selected for deportation. He was put on the *Arandora Star* too. I suppose it does show a certain consistency in the selection procedures. That's about all that *can* be said for it. When the officials on the *Arandora Star* saw the name Simon Treidel appear twice on the passenger list, they just assumed that it was a typing error.'

'And because of this "typing error",' I said bitterly, 'Stefan Treiber is dead.'

Carlton nodded.

'Well, you still haven't explained why I was followed and interrogated, and why you set up my meeting with Antonin Treiber.'

'First of all, I categorically deny that I "set you up" in the way that you describe. If Aubrey Taylor wants to concoct stories, then that's his business. I can hardly be blamed for it.' He seemed to have recovered from his contrition. 'As to your being followed and interrogated, that was a routine part of the investigation into Treiber's escape. You don't seem to realize the seriousness of a situation like that. This country is a fortress. Every single person within the fortress must be harnessed to the national effort. Either that, or they must be put under proper control.' (I looked forward to passing that Churchillian gem on to MacCready.) 'Once it was apparent that Treiber had gone missing – a German-speaking alien who in his business career had worked in radio communications – then no stone could be left unturned in hunting him down. Clearly the focus was on you and on Peter Musgrave, as the original sponsors of his immigration into the country.'

'You're forgetting that he *hadn't* escaped from the train,' I said. 'He was dead.'

'But we didn't know that. We couldn't take any risks. Anyway, as soon as the truth was discovered, a few days ago, the investigation was called off.'

'That was generous of you. And what about Antonin? Where's he?'

'We don't know. The police didn't even know he was in that basement. They've had nothing to do with him. Of course, we were told when he absconded from the family he was staying with. The police were watching out for him, particularly in view of the uncle's supposed escape. But they never found him.'

For a big man, he drank his tea with incongruously tiny, nervous sips. Between sips he glanced in my direction, gauging my reaction. I no longer knew what or whom to believe. The story of the 'typing error' was ridiculous enough to be true. On the other hand I could see no reason why Taylor should have got involved in the business apart from at the instigation of Carlton, despite the fact that Carlton didn't seem to be the suave deceiver of Taylor's imagination. Rather than accept a part of Carlton's story and not the rest, I rejected the lot.

On the way out of Christopher Carlton's club, I bought the *Evening Standard*. It was full of stuff about the last few nights' raids – tales of derring-do, fortitude under fire, those funny-things-that-happen-e'en-in-the-midst-of-tragedy. All the talk on the bus was like that too – frenetic, with perfect strangers pouring stories out to each other. Everyone was trying to prove that *they* had come closer than anyone else to being hit by a bomb. (Those who really had come closest, of course, weren't there to speak.) It was as though they didn't quite believe in the war; they wanted to bring it closer. There was a disgusting excitement in their voices, a relish in it all. A man beside me was saying to anyone who would listen: 'Bomb went past our place last night. Know what happened? The bloody phone starts ringing. It sets them off, you know. We'd heard one fall just a few streets away, and the wife, she was getting to feel a bit funky. Then there's this flash and another one comes down, and our bloody telephone starts ringing.'

'Didn't you answer it?' asked a woman with a scarf over her head. 'Might 'ave been Adolf on the line!' Everybody laughed, then someone else muscled in with their own anecdote, and so it went on, round and round the chorus of citizens. Hanging on each other's words, gabbling and clutching at each other, screaming with laughter, they worked themselves into a lather of awe at their own vulnerability and at the power of the bomb. I hated it. Oppressed by the claustrophobia of it all, I retreated into the 'News in Brief' column of the newspaper.

RUNNING RIOT

Cattle and sheep awaiting slaughter at an abattoir in Romford were given a brief reprieve yesterday when the building was hit by a stray bomb off-loaded by a German plane returning from a raid on London. The blast destroyed the outer wall of the yard in which the animals were penned. A number of beasts were killed and injured, and the rest panicked and burst out of their pens and on to the road. 'The animals stampeded down the street,' said Peter Cudlip, who works at the abattoir, 'but after a while they calmed down and we were able to round them up. They're safely back inside now.'

MYSTERY GRAFFITI

Police are investigating the appearance of Nazi swastikas among mysterious graffiti appearing outside Underground stations. The graffiti, featuring abstract swirls and circular patterns, has been found scratched into the entrances to Bethnal Green, Aldgate and Bank stations. A police spokesman refused to comment on speculation that the graffiti are coded messages being passed between fifth columnists. 'We are taking the matter very seriously,' he said.

DOWN THE DRAIN

The Cock public house in Bromsgrove Crescent, Wimbledon was destroyed in a raid last night, and the entire stock of drink was lost. Fortunately, the pub was closed at the time, and no one was injured. 'It was a tragedy,' said local resident Dennis Pole. 'There were rivers of Scotch running down the street, but none of it could be saved. When the fire started, the whole place went up like a rocket. I'd been going there for twenty years.'

The bus snaked its way to Kings Cross. So many streets had been roped off because of unexploded bombs that getting from the bus stop to my flat – a distance of only a few hundred yards – was like trying to find your way to the heart of a maze. I drank two whiskies when I finally got in, and phoned Musgrave. I told him what Carlton had told me – that Stefan Treiber had not escaped, but had been sent aboard the *Arandora Star* by mistake. I told him that I didn't believe this. Musgrave was 'utterly horrified' that such a mistake could have occurred. It confirmed everything that he had always said about the slapdash and arbitrary way in which these important decisions concerning internment and deportation had been made. I repeated that I didn't believe what Carlton had told me. I pointed out that since the authorities had lied once – I certainly didn't believe that it had only just been 'discovered' that Treiber had not in fact escaped but had been put on the *Arandora Star* – then there was no reason to think that they wouldn't lie again. Musgrave pointed out that even if one accepted that the authorities had deliberately lied in the first place, which he did not, it was nonsensical to suppose that they would merely compound the situation by adding a second lie. It was difficult to choose between our two forms of logic. After a brief argument about it, during which he claimed that I was showing signs of paranoia, we hung up.

I had been slipping deeper and deeper into boozy chaos ever since the bombing began. The floor of my flat was thick with unwashed plates, unopened mail, unread papers, unfinished books. I began shovelling things into piles, stacking the crockery in the kitchen and putting the books back on the shelves. Among them were the two that Antonin had been looking at. The first, I discovered, was a travel book on Central Europe, with photographs of mountain scenery, cathedrals, town squares and cattle being paraded down village streets. The second was *Art and Rituals of Primitive Peoples* by Margery Forester, 'with 15 pages of plates and 50 line illustrations'. It lay open at the page I imagined Antonin to have been looking at when the authorities burst in and snatched him away. I picked it up and began reading.

Figs. 26–50. The spiral is one of the most potent of symbolic forms among primitive peoples. It is to be found adorning the entrances to tombs and labyrinths from Ireland to India, by way of Iraq. It is associated with death, and with a return to the womb.

Above this were a number of spiral forms – some were single-lined coils, others had arms radiating from a central point. Above them were various swastikas (Figs. 21–25) 'from the Hindu word for "good luck".' No. 25 was the gammadion, whose radiating arms were like those of some of the spirals below, but frozen into solid right-angles. I gazed at these drawings for a long time, my eyes spinning round and round, and as I did so a memory of something I had read struggled to the surface of my hungover, boozed-out brain. I dropped the book and grabbed the copy of the *Evening Standard* that was wedged into the pocket of my raincoat.

XII

Ripples

So ANTONIN TREIBER was out there somewhere. I could see him crawling alone through the blackout, scratching those pathetic signals. I could see him loitering at the entrances to the Underground, hesitating to go down because he feared the mass of foreigners down there, feared how they would react to a Jew boy, an alien, coming down to breathe their air. I could see him look back over his shoulder, listening to the bombs come closer, then slink down the steps.

I had no doubts that the graffiti were messages to me. Hungry and denied the use of language, the only means of expression that came to him were those swirls and symbols that he associated with his last moments of comfort and security before being snatched from my flat. These scratched symbols formed the Ariadne's thread that pulled me in turn through the labyrinth of London's Underground. I began at Bethnal Green, where the scratchings were still plainly to be seen on the wall outside the station. The swastika had been so defaced as to be hardly visible. (How confused and desperate the boy must have been to draw *that*! I could imagine the crowds that milled around outside, that slumped down below in the fetid tunnels, stringing him from a pub sign, or throwing him in front of the trains that rattled through the station, for drawing *that*.) At Bethnal Green I studied every face in the queue (bad teeth, the women's hair greying and falling out, complexions of putty and cement) but didn't find him. I took the train to Bank, staring at the blankness of the boarded-up windows. At Liverpool Street the doors slid open like stage curtains to reveal bright lights, children running up and down, a couple playing cards, women arranging bedding. Then the doors closed, the show was over, the train rumbled on.

At Bank I stumbled through all the corridors and platforms. The next night I went to Aldgate and waited outside in the dark while the bombers rumbled high above me. Nothing. The Treiber boy was nowhere to be found. I scoured the entrances to other stations – Moorgate, Liverpool Street, Holborn, Farringdon – and found the marks that told me he had passed through these as well. Scratched into the portals of the entrances – just as they had been scratched on the entrances to tombs thousands of years ago, according to Professor Forester – were scrolls, spirals and swirls, and occasionally the rigid arms of a swastika. Sometimes they were so faint that they could hardly be made out with the naked eye. I took to carrying a magnifying glass with me, flipping my spectacles on to my forehead and bending down close to the grimy walls. People began to pass comments, and one night at Farringdon a policeman took me into the booking office and demanded to know why I was snooping around the station.

I spread my net wider, to Elephant & Castle and Clapham in the South, to Oxford Circus and Kensington in the West. The deeper stations of the Northern Line were most popular with the shelterers. Down there the bombs could not even be heard and life survived in a warm, cramped, womb-like capsule. At Aldwych and at Elephant & Castle, where the current was switched off, makeshift hammocks were sometimes slung between the raised rails. Coats and hats hung from the round walls. Naked arms fell across the bellies of strangers, and their fingers twitched and fidgeted in their sleep. The only sound in the depths of the night was of collective breathing, like a wind blowing. Inside the tunnel was a herd of humanity.

So it went on for weeks, while autumn dragged itself into a damp and bitter winter. The floating brick dust and deep sunsets of the early Blitz were replaced by mud – splattered everywhere in great clods where a bomb had dropped – and the rich smell of fresh, wet earth in the air. By day I was part of that world, struggling in to work at the Ministry every day, and at night I descended into that other world where humanity gathered as if in the hold of a ship and was rocked to and fro on an ocean of sleep. I searched that other world from end to end, up and down the emergency stairs, along the platforms, through the corridors and entrance halls that multiplied like branches of a tree, like the proliferation of plots in a nineteenth-century novel.

And then one night, a night of terrible bombing, I was standing just inside the entrance to St Paul's station, watching a building opposite burn. Flames were shooting horizontally from the windows. Millions of embers floated down out of the black sky like electric snow. As the fire tore away the flesh of the building, it exposed, like ribs, the big iron girders of the roof. Every now and then, among the crackle of flames, there was a crash of falling brick and glass. I had been enjoying this magnificent spectacle for a while, thinking vaguely that I ought to go underground (the bombers were bound to use it as a target), when I happened to look to my right down Cheapside. About a hundred and fifty yards away, crouched against the wall with his back to me, lit by the glow of the burning building, was a figure. I called Antonin's name, and the figure sprang up and turned to me. The fire across the road gusted up and roared. As I started down the pavement, calling 'Antonin! Antonin!', the figure turned and started running down Cheapside. I followed. As I ran past the place where he had been crouching, I thought I could see those familiar swirls carved into the wall. Everything seemed to have come full circle. I felt that same sense of theatre as I had when I lost Taylor outside the public shelter. Antonin's coat flapped about him as he disappeared over the lip of the road. I stumbled forward, almost in a crouching position, shouting to him to stop. The burning buildings burst into applause. Ahead of me, Antonin ran through a strange river of steam and smoke that flowed along the ground. I saw a couple of firemen come out of a side street and wade into it up to their knees, dragging the nozzle of a hose. It looked like the head of a snake. We ran on past them. There was the strangest sense of running through a river you cannot feel. It was like being blown by a wind that never touches you. All the time I was shouting to Antonin to stop, not to be afraid. As we came up Poultry towards Mansion House he was getting further and further ahead.

Before I heard it, I sensed the violence of the bomb, the motion of it hurtling in to earth as though sucked in by a magnet. The sound, which was deafening, was somewhere between an enormous piece of paper being ripped and the screech of water disappearing down a plug hole. My legs went soft and gave way, and I felt the muscles of my bowels and sphincter relax.

The splat, splat of mud falling around me. I had mud in my mouth, mud up my nose. I cradled my head in my arms, cheek against the wet tarmac. When everything was quiet, I looked up. At the point where I had last seen Antonin Treiber, at the junction between the Bank of England and Mansion House, the road had collapsed into the Underground station below. I stood, shaken and soiled, at the edge of the crater. The tangled ends of pipes, drains and cables hung out where the road had sheared away. The blast of the bomb had sliced through these sinews of the city. Seeping through the smell of fresh, wet earth was the stink of escaping gas. I looked down into the crater, called feebly, pointlessly for Antonin. It was remarkably still down there – just a sound of water and the hiss of the escaping gas. Then noise, activity behind me. Fire appliances, ambulances, rescue workers were beginning to arrive. A couple of policemen, clearing the area of sightseers, hustled me away.

I read the details of the 'incident' in the papers over the next few days. One hundred and eleven people were killed. Some had been in the ticket office just below the road. Others had been blown off the platform into the path of a train. I made enquiries with the police and the hospitals, but none of them knew of a sixteen-year-old boy caught in the blast. At nights I dreamt of him running over the rim of the crater. I watched him fall, spinning and screaming down that black hole. That loop went round and round.

I stopped drinking. Somehow I hung on to my job. I thought I might be going mad. I began to doubt whether it really was Antonin Treiber that I had chased down Cheapside or whether he really had fallen into the crater. I took to trudging round the Underground stations again, giving people descriptions of Antonin and asking whether they had seen him. A shell-shocked soldier rambled to me about how he thought he might have been with him weeks before – but he was only saying it, it transpired, as an excuse to tell war stories. The graffiti continued to appear, but less and less often, as though they were radio signals whose source was moving further and further away. Sometimes they were so faint as to be barely decipherable. I had to trace over them myself with a piece of broken glass, and I soon came to wonder whether it wasn't in fact me who was drawing them.

They grew fainter and fainter, and then disappeared. One way or another, Antonin Treiber had been swallowed up completely. The signals had died.

XIII

Final Twists

WEEKS LATER, I was informed by the police that there was after all an adolescent male – 'circumcised penis, dark hair' – among the unidentified bodies from the Bank station incident. The legs had been ripped off in the blast. I went to a morgue in Battersea and identified the discoloured, frozen face of Antonin Treiber. It had the same expression of helpless repose and vulnerability as the sleepers in the Underground. For some reason, seeing it made me more inclined to believe that the uncle too was dead, that the tangled story of the 'typing error' had been true after all. I spent weeks in depression, mulling over the Treiber case – two innocents swallowed up by Musgrave's 'good war'. Never before had I felt so oppressively the claustrophobia of being inside the snail.

I had drifted a long way from the world, from Taylor and Musgrave and MacCready. I had made my own internal migration. But in a distant, disconnected way, I still kept track of what was happening outside myself. For Musgrave, despite the insouciance he had affected with me, the news of Stefan Treiber's death aboard the *Arandora Star* had had a galvanising effect. Now he had the perfect weapon of revenge against Carlton, an instrument that, if handled correctly, could destroy his rival's political career. For the tangled story of the 'typing error', that catalogue of mishaps whereby Stefan Treiber had drowned off the Irish Coast, 'revealed administrative incompetence and disregard of elementary civil-service procedures of a most appalling magnitude.' (I followed his speeches in Hansard.) The minister ultimately responsible for these bunglings was the old enemy, Christopher Carlton.

Musgrave went about his task assiduously. He put down motions, tabled questions, jumped up to catch the Speaker's eye on every possible occasion. He generally made as much of a nuisance of himself as he could on the subject of the *Arandora Star* and the procedures that had been followed in selecting internees for deportation. All his questions were of a general nature, mentioning no names or specifics, but (as he revealed to me later) he had let it be known to Carlton through private channels – there was no harm in putting the wind up him – that that could change. Members of Parliament had got used to hearing Peter Musgrave on the subject of refugees – it had become 'his' issue – but this new flurry of activity attracted attention. People could smell a rat. Carlton's stock in the tearooms began to fall. (Not, of course, that Musgrave put such a cynical construction on his own actions. In his own eyes he was merely acting in the public interest. If that happened to advance his own career and destroy that of his enemy, then that was merely natural justice, a tribute to the soundness and self-righting instincts of the British Constitution.)

Carlton seemed to buckle under this pressure. Musgrave told me later that Carlton had invited him for talks 'so that he could set his [Musgrave's] mind at rest on certain points'. Musgrave rejected these overtures, replying that if Carlton had anything to say he should be 'man enough to make a public statement in the House'. He kept this fastidiousness up right through the damp and bitter winter, well into '41. He only relented, I suspected, when it became clear that the *Arandora Star* was fading from the collective memory of the House of Commons tearoom. With no further advantage to be had from keeping Carlton on the rack, Musgrave agreed to talk to him in private. Perhaps in order to put extra pressure on him, he phoned me to ask me to attend as well.

Of course, I jumped at the opportunity. We met at the Ministry, where there were wide expanses of green leather on desks and of brown leather on bookcases. An official sat silently in the corner of the room, notepad on knee.

'You've given me a hell of a run-around over this internment business,' Carlton began, to Musgrave. (He ignored me for most of the interview. The way he talked to Musgrave was quite different from the way he had addressed me.) 'I have got other things to do, you know. Dare I say it, more important things.'

'I would have thought the deaths of six hundred people were quite important. Wouldn't you?'

'Of course. But in your wholly admirable enthusiasm for our Jewish friends, you seem to forget that we are fighting a war, and that security considerations must be paramount. This country is a fortress. Every single person within the fortress must be harnessed to the national effort. Either that, or they must be put under proper control.'

'You can't get away with that, Chris. You've accepted that Stefan Treiber was never involved in spying. He never escaped from internment.'

'Yes, but the fact is that there are still security considerations involved.'

'How can there be? Treiber wasn't a spy.'

'There are *other* security considerations.'

Musgrave was silent for a moment. 'What considerations?'

'That is what I have asked you here to tell you. Naturally,

it is covered by the Official Secrets Act.' He glared meaningfully at me. 'I'm afraid I lied when I said that Stefan Treiber was among those drowned aboard the *Arandora Star*. I'm sure you'll agree, when you hear what I have to say, that I did it for good reasons. Mr Treiber is in fact alive and well. He was among those who survived the sinking of the *Arandora Star*. Some of those on upper decks managed to make it to the lifeboats before the ship went down. When the survivors of that tragic event were brought back to England, MI5 and the SIS took a number of them under their wing, so to speak, with a view to using them as spies. Their "death" in the Atlantic would provide a perfect cover for a change of identity, prior to being used either as double-agents here, or for espionage in occupied territory. We would be mad not to use such a pool of German and Italian speakers.'

'So Stefan Treiber *is* a spy,' said Musgrave, 'but for us?'

'Unfortunately not. He turned out to be unsuitable. MI5 considered that he didn't have the mental aptitude for spying. He was rejected. But having been a party to MI5 vetting procedures, not to mention the whole scheme to use *Arandora Star* survivors as spies, he clearly could not be simply released back into the community. He, and other cases like his, are to be kept in secure quarantine for the duration of the war. Officially, they don't exist.'

'And Treiber's presence on the ship,' I asked, 'that was a genuine mistake?'

'Absolutely. The story of the "typing error" – all that's true. Regrettable, of course, but quite true. We really did think that he had escaped. Then when he turned up among the survivors of the *Arandora Star* and MI5 took him under their wing, they decided to maintain the story. A story like that could only support his credibility as a double-agent.'

'But an escape like that could easily be arranged. It would

be unlikely to succeed *without* being arranged. Surely the Germans would realize that.'

'Perhaps, perhaps not. It hardly matters now.'

'What about the surveillance of my house in London?' said Musgrave. 'What about Special Branch interrogating Morgan and following me around? How do you justify all that if you knew all along that he hadn't escaped?'

'But Peter,' said Carlton with affronted innocence, 'you forget that he was being considered as possible counter-espionage material. He had to be thoroughly vetted. Every conceivable area of his background had to be investigated, and that included yourself and Morgan. Clearly we were worried because his nephew had disappeared. We wanted to make absolutely sure there wasn't something fishy going on. Of course, when Treiber proved to be unsuitable material, we called off the investigation.'

'How were the Germans to know of this miraculous escape?' I said. 'It was long enough before I got to hear of it.'

'Perhaps they're better at keeping up with the provincial press than you.' He pushed a page of newspaper across the green leather. It was page three of the *Bristol Evening News* for July 3rd, 1940. Tucked away in the bottom left-hand corner was the following item:

MAN HUNT

Police are searching for Stefan Treiber, a Czech internee who disappeared yesterday from a train carrying internees to a transit camp in Bristol. Police describe him as in his fifties, tall and stooping, with thin grey hair and blue eyes. He speaks English with a foreign accent. He should not be approached, and any sightings should be reported to the police.

'And it's popular reading in Berlin, is it,' said Musgrave, 'the *Bristol Evening News?*'

Carlton smiled. 'Goebbels reads little else, I'm told.' They were both amused.

'I want to see Treiber,' I said. It annoyed me to hear them bantering complacently.

'I'm afraid that's out of the question,' said Carlton. 'MI5 have placed him in safe quarantine. They would never agree to the quarantine being breached.'

'Has he been told about his nephew's death?'

'I've no idea. I doubt it. I would imagine that would constitute a breach of quarantine.'

'I think he should be told. I want to see Treiber for myself. You'll forgive me if I'm rather sceptical about this latest story of yours.'

Carlton was adamant that I would not be allowed to see Treiber. We argued about it for a while. Musgrave, who seemed to regard the matter as now being settled, said nothing on either side. I walked out in a temper.

That, I thought, would be the end of the affair. If Treiber really was alive, I would have to wait until the end of the war before I could see him. But who knew how long the war would last? And would the old man still be alive at the end of it? The strong, obscure guilt I felt over the Treibers continued to gnaw at me.

But a fortnight later, Christopher Carlton phoned to tell me that he had made enquiries and that I would, after all, be allowed to visit Stefan Treiber. Perhaps he still thought, mistakenly, that I could make trouble for him.

XIV

The Dreams

W AS it guilt? Certainly, some vast, unnameable emotion
had been drawn into me by the circumstances of the
Treiber case, and in particular by the fate of the boy, Antonin
Treiber. Hate of the war – this 'good war' – and of this
damp fortress, England, was something to do with it. And
beyond that, encompassing that, was a feeling that the dead
boy might hold some secret intended for me, that he might
even represent a point of rest, an end to the internal
migration that was taking me further and further from the
war, from the world. I can't explain it, but I felt a burning
desire to know something of what was at the centre, to
know anything of the boy about whom so much seemed to
revolve. It seemed that any scrap of information might make
everything else mean something – even the war, which held
reality in its iron grip. In my imagination the boy had
become a world within the war. The spirals he had drawn
at the entrances to the Underground no longer seemed to be
cries for help, but a signal meant to guide me – as though
Antonin Treiber, like Taylor, was saying to me, 'You need
me.' And I believed him.

There was curiosity, of course. Two mysteries remained in the Treiber business, one of which concerned Taylor's story that Carlton had told him to arrange for me to meet the boy. Carlton continued to deny this, claiming that though the security services had had Widlake Street under observation, they had not seen Antonin Treiber there. When I pressed him on this, he even implied that the boy's presence at the house had been a figment of my imagination. All this was no more than I expected, for it was unlikely that Carlton would admit to a deliberate attempt to implicate myself and Musgrave in the affair. Yet if Carlton knew that Stefan Treiber wasn't a spy, if the whole exercise was simply one of vetting him, then there was nothing to be implicated in and no reason for Carlton to have had me taken to the boy. Perhaps, after all, it was just another of Taylor's fantasies, or perhaps MacCready and Taylor had contrived the whole thing as some kind of practical joke. I was inclined to reject this and believe instead that Taylor had indeed received instructions from Carlton and that Carlton had some deeper, hidden motive for this. Perhaps Carlton – envisaging Stefan Treiber's death? – was, after all, manufacturing a story that linked Musgrave, myself and the Treibers in some kind of spying conspiracy. There seemed no end to the possible machinations and no way of resolving their mystery. It would remain, for the moment, a loose end dangling before me.

Although it concerned my own original involvement in the Treiber affair, this question of whether and why Taylor had taken me to Widlake Street faded in my mind before the second mystery: what had Antonin Treiber himself been doing there? The machinations of Carlton, Musgrave, Mac-Cready and Taylor seemed dry and cerebral compared with this, the human question at their centre. Again I found myself brought back to the boy himself. Who was he?

So it was curiosity and something bigger than curiosity

that made me so anxious to see Stefan Treiber. I obtained an assurance from Carlton that I would be the one to break to him the news of his nephew's death. Perhaps I thought his reaction might tell me something about the boy. Perhaps I wished to assuage my guilt. In some insane way I really thought I was making a new start. The journey by train to see him inflamed these feelings – it was the first time I'd been out of the city since the beginning of the Blitz. As soon as the last suburbs had disappeared backwards into the silver drizzle, I felt an unexpected sense of freedom and possibility.

The institution where Stefan Treiber was being held, in the West Country, was something between a lunatic asylum and a prison. The authorities presumably judged that anybody Treiber might communicate with there would either think he was mad or be mad themselves. He had been renamed Steven Trevor.

The hospital, as it was called, was a large Edwardian mansion set in wooded grounds. (During the course of our conversation, Treiber remarked that it reminded him of living in Musgrave's house in Sussex.) The atmosphere inside was damp and chilly. The windows were barred, and the tables and chairs chained to the floor, as though it were a ship.

Treiber looked much as he had when I last saw him, two years before. The hair was a shade whiter, perhaps, but otherwise he was remarkably unchanged. I suppose I was expecting the traumas he had been through to have left some kind of mark. If they had, it was only in that he was even more still, more disconnected, than I remember him being. I studied him very closely when he was led into the reception room to meet me, and I use the word 'disconnected' almost in a literal sense. For it was as though all the things that had happened to him – the railway crash some eight years before, the flight from Czechoslovakia, internment, the sinking of the *Arandora Star* – had one by one snapped the vital connections that had kept him joined to the world. His blue eyes, when they looked at you, were veiled behind films of moisture. Not tears, but a membrane that separated his world from everything else. It was as though he had slipped his moorings and drifted out on to a calm sea.

The interior of the 'hospital' – painted the same greyish pink as Inspector Saville's interview room – was unutterably depressing, so I suggested to Treiber that we should walk in the grounds. To my surprise, nobody had been assigned to listen to our conversation – indeed the place seemed to be quite deserted apart from the man who had checked my papers at the gate and the receptionist. Treiber agreed to my suggestion with a faint nod and a smile that was little more than another veil drawn over his face.

The drizzle outside was a light mist of moisture that made the grass and trees seem closer and more tactile. We walked across a broad lawn – Treiber lagging a pace or two at my side – towards a line of trees. I was asking him polite, inconsequential questions about how he was being treated, to which he smiled vaguely and nodded or shook his head. I had introduced myself – in case he had forgotten who I was – but although I am sure he recognized me instantly, he registered no surprise, curiosity or pleasure.

The line of trees turned out to be a dense plantation of conifers, crisscrossed by silent, needle-carpeted paths. I noticed that Treiber shuffled awkwardly, scuffing his feet through the brown pine needles. Pine cones were strewn along the path like handgrenades. I savoured for a few moments longer that pleasure of being the bearer of bad tidings. I suggested that we rest for a few moments on a log that appeared surrealistically to have been placed beside the path to accommodate us. We sat down.

'Stefan,' I said, 'I'm afraid you must prepare yourself for a shock. I've come here to break the news to you that your nephew is dead. Antonin was killed in an air raid in London in January.' I paused, then added, 'I am sorry.'

I was watching him all the time as I said this – he sat beside me on the log, tall and staring straight ahead into the conifers. When I reached the words 'your nephew is dead' (the words seemed to roll forward of their own volition, detaching themselves from me) I saw his whole body contract as though he were slowly wincing. His head dropped down into his shoulders and his shoulders sank. He was like a mollusc withdrawing into its shell. He turned his head to me and said, more as a statement than a question, 'There can be no doubt about this.'

It seemed a strange thing to say. It reminded me – uncannily, irrelevantly – of MacCready's comment on my meeting the boy in Widlake Street: 'So you do know him.'

'I saw the body myself,' I replied. 'It was him.'

Treiber bowed his head and pinched the bridge of his nose, as though he were suffering from a headache. I observed this quite dispassionately. Two tears, without touching his cheeks, fell straight on to the pine needles below. I turned away, embarrassed. Somehow I had not been expecting a show of grief.

'He was only a boy,' he said.

The banality of this remark shocked me. It was almost vulgar. I stayed silent, feeling ashamed. When a few minutes had passed, and more tears had fallen on the forest floor, I said, 'What was he like? What kind of a boy was he?' Then I added, shamelessly, 'It might help you to talk about him.'

'He was just a *boy*,' said Treiber irritably. 'How can you ask what he was *like*? His life was hardly begun. He was my nephew, he liked to draw, he was a sweet boy. Nothing. His life had not begun.' He stood up, as though he wanted to leave me.

'Please,' I said, and stood up too. 'Let's walk a bit further. I've come a long way to talk to you.'

He shrugged his shoulders and followed alongside me further into the forest.

'I've been told everything that's happened to you since you were interned,' I said. I was disgusted at the tone of apology that had found its way into my voice, as though I partook of some collective guilt.

'The English think they are very superior and very clever,' said Treiber. 'I hope they win this war, but not as much as I wish that it had never happened.' He paused, then added, 'I think some of the English are rather happy about their war.'

It pleased me that he did not seemed to include me among 'the English'. Whether he had noticed my traces of a Welsh accent or whether he was no longer thinking about me one way or another, I couldn't tell.

'The Englishmen who interrogated me when I returned from the sea seemed very happy with the war,' he continued. 'They told me that I lacked the right "character" to work for them. I think they hoped by their questions to peel me layer by layer until they found the right "character" underneath. That was the purpose of their questions. Anyway, I failed the test, for which I am glad.

'The English are great believers in "character", I think. Perhaps they hope that "character" will win this war for them? Myself, I don't believe so much in "character". We are what we experience. That is what I mean when I say that my nephew was just a boy, that he was nothing. Perhaps I shocked you? But if you take all the layers of experience off a man, you find no nut at the centre, no "character". He is like an onion, all layers and no centre.'

As he said this, I looked at him and tried to imagine him on the sinking *Arandora Star*, perhaps scrambling on to a lifeboat as the ship heaved beneath him. I couldn't do it. His words and manner were empty, as though the real activity of his mind were unreachable, taking place somewhere far off.

'But you must be able to tell me *something* about Antonin,' I said. 'You must have talked together.'

'Of course we talked. He told me many things. He told me of his hopes for the future. But what has become of those words now? They're gone, nothing. The boy is dead.

'I'm sorry. I am speaking angrily, but none of this is your fault, Mr Morgan. The boy missed his parents very much.'

Ahead of us down the path on which we were walking was the tall perimeter fence of the hospital's grounds. I guided Treiber to the right, down a path that took us further into the forest.

'Perhaps I do remember one or two things, Mr Morgan. And perhaps you are right, it is good to talk about the boy. You see, he used to tell me about his dreams. He lived a limited life. He was an only child. Even at home in Prague, he never played much with other children. His dreams came to be of great interest to him, perhaps as a kind of play.

'So when we found ourselves alone together in England, he would tell me about all the dreams that he had had. Perhaps I should say that I had never been close to him back home. I have never been comfortable with children and never had any of my own. We were thrown together by circumstance. Most of these dreams of his were of no conse-quence, just projections of childish desires. But there were two that stuck in my mind, though I could not say what my "explanation" of them might be. They were both dreams that he had had repeatedly, both here and when he was back at home.

'The first concerned a giant who was eating up all his friends. As I have said, Antonin did not have any friends of his own age, so these dream friends must have been invented. His bedroom was at the top of a flight of stairs in one wing of the house. His parents were quite wealthy and they had a large house in Prague. These stairs went down to a central landing, and then there were stairs down from that landing to the hall and the dining room. Antonin dreamt that his parents were having a big party. I can imagine this myself, as my brother and sister-in-law were enthusiastic hosts and often organized large gatherings of journalists and suchlike. All the grown-ups were down in the dining room, and their children, Antonin's imaginary friends, were sleeping together in Antonin's room. There were camp beds spread out across the floor. Or at least they were meant to be sleeping, but in fact they lay awake in the dark and chattered excitedly, pausing sometimes to listen to the comforting hum of their parents' party down below. But then a giant came to the house. Antonin told me he could see him coming, striding across a fairy-tale landscape, but he was powerless to do anything to stop him. The giant got into the house and sat on the landing between the children and their parents. Then he reached his arm up the stairs and thrust his hand into Antonin's bedroom. One by one he picked Antonin's friends out of their beds and ate them. He would take one and withdraw his arm to eat the child. Then he would thrust his hand in again for another one. Of course, there was much screaming and confusion in the bedroom, but the parents downstairs in the dining room couldn't hear what was happening above the sound of the party. Antonin's bed was in the corner furthest from the door, and he cowered against the wall and screamed as he watched the hand come in again and again to take his friends to be eaten.

'Perhaps you can imagine how frightening this dream would be for a young boy. He told me that he would wake up from it crying, cowering against the wall exactly like he did in the dream. I have often puzzled as to the meaning of it. Clearly there is a sense of separation from his parents, perhaps even a feeling of betrayal in the way his cries for help go unheard. Sometimes I think that that giant, coming between him and his parents, threatening to devour him, was the war itself. Of course, he dreamed all this before the war, before the war seemed even likely. But I do not think that that is necessarily an objection. Perhaps you share the English "commonsense", and will laugh at this, but I have read that our dreams are not governed by the same rules as our conscious lives. Our dreams can reflect experiences gathered from the future. Perhaps this is so. I am prepared to believe it. What else do children dream of? When new-born babies twitch and cry out in their sleep, what else can they be dreaming about?

'The second dream of Antonin's that stuck in my mind is not so eventful, but from the way he described it to me, I think it was even more terrifying. It is really more of a single vision than a story. He is in a small boat, a rowing boat, being rowed across a limitless sea by a creature. The creature is upright and reptilian, with enormous, nocturnal eyes. It sits opposite Antonin and rows him, staring at him, across the dark sea. The sea that laps at the sides of the boat is pure black, like ink. Everything else, the sky, is angry, a terrifying red and purple. Ahead there is only darkness. Antonin told me that what he remembered most, what terrified him most, was the ceaseless rocking motion of the small boat on this black ocean. The two saucer eyes of the creature opposite him stared motionlessly into his, but the boat itself rocked from side to side without end. Antonin told me that he would wake from this dream bathed in sweat and would continue to feel that rocking motion for hours after.'

We had come to a halt, staring ahead of us down the path into the wet conifers. But this was no epiphany. The old man's chatter about dreams passed me by. It was clear he could tell me nothing about the boy. I was trying to remember the way out of the plantation, so that I could get the old man back to the hospital. It was unpleasantly damp now, and Treiber's voice, with the twist of its central European accent, was beginning to get on my nerves. And besides, I had a train to catch.

XV

An End

Wᴵᴛʜ ᴀ ʟᴀꜱᴛ terrible raid on May 10, which killed four-teen hundred people, the Blitz came to an end. Hitler turned his gaze on Russia. During the weeks that followed my visit to Stefan Treiber, Aubrey Taylor continued to send me some of his manuscripts – the gloomy poems, the stories on quasi-mythological themes, soaked in imagery of cruci-fixion, blood and darkness. Perhaps he still hoped that I might somehow help to get them published. He described himself as a 'New Apocalyptic'. Apocalypse, he wrote, was 'a universal cleansing, an achievement of organic synthesis between spirit and matter, myth and history, individual and universal – a breaking down of the barriers of consciousness. Man is a tree.' Most of the packages I left unopened and they accumulated in tottering piles beside the door of my flat.

After the end of the bombing, I started drinking again at the Belgravia Tavern. Nothing had changed there since the dark winter. Most of the faces were different, the picture shaken by the comings and goings of war. But they whirled around on that sea of beer in the same way. The same eddies formed around the same house eccentrics – the philandering poets, the professional shirkers and the self-proclaimed anarchists. MacCready was still there, surrounded by his group of admirers, and Taylor was more than ever a member of that group. He was always arguing with MacCready about Art, his nervous, obsessive eyes forever scouring the Scotsman's scowling face. Taylor had stopped sending his work to me by this time, as MacCready became the sole object of his attentions. When we ran into each other in the Belgravia, he greeted me perfunctorily, always glancing round to see what MacCready was doing. He talked about MacCready incessantly.

I tended to avoid both of them, because their presence reminded me too much of the terrible business of Antonin Treiber. I had formed new acquaintanceships on the outer, more staid circles of the Belgravia universe, and it was with them that I would pass the beer-sodden evenings. One night, however, I did go up and talk to MacCready and Taylor. I had not noticed MacCready setting up a stall of his pipe-cleaner animals on the bar. It reminded me of the start of the whole thing – that evening the previous September when MacCready had taken me back to his basement to meet the boy.

I stood chatting to MacCready at the bar about his models, while Taylor watched us silently. The models now fell into two categories. Some were crassly realistic – round-eyed puppies and curled-up kittens like the nauseating knick-knacks you might have picked up on Brighton or Hastings pier in peacetime. Some of these, the more expensive, were painted. (He'd turned these out, he told me, in a desperate bid to make some money.) But at the other extreme, his stylised, bolder models had become more abstract than ever. The baroque trunk of the elephant had grown grotesquely out of proportion, billowing up from the stumpy legs in rolling waves. At the end of the row of animals, the snail had a weird, shimmering quality, as though it were in fact two snails fighting or making love, or as though the viewer were drunk and seeing double. (Or perhaps, as we were all drunk that night, one should say sober and seeing single.)

'Of course,' said Taylor, pointing into the inside of the snail, where the coils died out, 'that shouldn't really have an end at all.'

'What the hell are you talking about?' asked MacCready aggressively.

Taylor gently picked up the snail, glancing at MacCready to see whether it was all right for him to do so. 'These swirls,' he said. 'The spiral should go on forever, twisting tighter and tighter, smaller and smaller, into infinity. And outwards, too it should swirl in ever-widening circles, encompassing more and more space. Instead, this just starts and stops. It can only hint at the truth of the spiral.'

'You're talking bloody rubbish,' said MacCready. 'And it'd better not be your twisted, mealy-mouthed, English way of saying you think my model's no good or I'll take these pipe-cleaners and make a spiral round your neck that really will get tighter and tighter.'

'You don't understand,' said Taylor. 'It would be impossible for any work of art to capture what I'm talking about. Imagine a film camera that goes into closer focus. It focuses on a spiral. The spiral gets smaller and smaller at the centre, until it can't be made out. The camera jumps to a closer shot, so that what was too small to make out before now fills the screen. But again the spiral goes on disappearing into the centre of the screen. So the camera jumps in again, further into the spiral, and each time, with each jump, the spiral disappears down the centre of the screen, like a tunnel going on for ever. Eternity. Chaos.'

'Sounds like a bloody boring film to me,' said MacCready.

'And the other way too,' Taylor continued eagerly. 'Imagine you're going the other way, out of the spiral, and the spiral ahead of you is getting wider and wider, taking in more and more space. It couldn't be done, of course, because the screen would have to get bigger and bigger. You could only look back and watch the spiral fall into place and close up behind you. Or perhaps coming out of the spiral would look the same as going in? And what about if you went on that journey for ever? Perhaps at some point you'd be back at the point where you started – except that you'd never started, because you'd been travelling for ever. You'd never know if or when you got to that point, or if you'd in fact always been at that point, because every point on the journey looks like every other.'

'And everything you say is starting to sound the same, Taylor,' said MacCready. 'Why don't you buy us a drink? That would sound different.'

'All I was trying to say,' said Taylor, sounding more ridiculous by the minute, 'was that your model illustrates an important thing about art. You see the reason that it can't represent the whole of the spiral, in its infinity, but only hint at it, is that it has to be cast in material form. The pipe-cleaners can only be bent so tight. It's trying to attain something non-material, something outside itself, but it's imprisoned in its material form. It's trapped in its materiality.'

'You know your trouble, Taylor?' said MacCready, pushing his glass on to the bar, slopping beer on to the curled-up cats. 'You're one of those people who secretly hates art. You just like thinking about it, destroying it with thought. You're like a man who'd rather have a wank than make love to a woman. This snail of mine is what it is – pipe-cleaners. The art is in how I've fashioned it, with my two hands, not in your flaccid daydreams about what you think it might be "trying to attain". Go on, Taylor, look at it. Feel it. Touch it. Can't do that any more, can you? All you can do is cocoon yourself in all that twaddle about infinite spirals, so that you don't have to face up to the fact that it exists. Do you know something, Taylor? I think this model of mine exists more than you do. You're so twisted, you're hardly there as flesh and blood. Go on, Taylor, feel how much more real it is than you.'

MacCready grabbed the snail from Taylor's hands and pulled it into one long stretched-out coil. He grabbed Taylor's arm and shoved it into the coil of pipe-cleaners – ranting all the time about how Taylor should feel it and how he was hardly real – so that it hung on Taylor's arm up to his elbow like a ridiculous bracelet. The people around us watched and laughed. I got the impression that MacCready and Taylor put on this kind of drunken floor show regularly. Taylor didn't take the coil off his arm, but kept arguing back. I was beginning to lose interest in these theatricals. Taylor was gabbling on about how MacCready had misunderstood him; how the idea of the spiral wasn't something detached from the model spiral, but was rather what it *was*; how the model snail wore its form on the outside, not concealed under its flesh, just as the snail itself wore its skeleton on the outside. MacCready, not listening to him, pursuing his own drunken path, told him not to be so bloody English, told him that he wouldn't know a real work of art if it wrapped itself around his private parts. The audience around them roared with laughter. Another night in the Belgravia.

Taylor gabbles on, spinning out his argument. In his desperation to be understood, to prove some obscure point to his convoluted discourse, he pulls a crumpled manuscript from his pocket. MacCready snatches it from him and begins reading in a booming, melodramatic voice: 'At the beginning of the show, the lights dim. The curtains, a river of blood from ceiling to floor, slowly slide apart . . .' He climbs up on to a chair to continue, exaggerating his expression to get laughs. '. . . eyes are wide open, as though they are buckets and the light from the screen a liquid that is being poured into them . . .'

In the story that MacCready reads, a boy is watching a film set in a forest. He imagines himself to be in the forest. As the story progresses, it turns out to be a grotesque, twisted variation on the Hansel and Gretel theme. The boy, lost in the film, in the forest, finds the sugared cottage and begins to eat it. The sugar is drugged, poisoned. The boy wanders away, leaving his trail of crumbs along the tracks of the forest. He is followed but never found. The trail of crumbs he leaves form an impossible labyrinth. He is lost forever in the depths of the forest, eating the poisoned sugar, eternally searching for a happy ending. The film never finishes. The national anthem is never played.